The Key to Greenvale

Philip J Williams

Copyright © 2024 Philip J Williams

All rights reserved.

DEDICATION

To all the fallen heroes, for whom the light of life no longer shines.

CONTENTS

1	Prologue	Pg 1
2	The key to Greenvale	Pg 2
3	A bird's eye view	Pg 9
4	Cleon's pride	Pg 11
5	Farewell salute	Pg 15
6	The company of wolves	Pg 17
7	Neighbours	Pg 20
8	The faithful	Pg 25
9	From tiny acorns grow…	Pg 29
10	The fall of man	Pg 38
11	Corporal Smith	Pg 44
12	The door	Pg 48
13	The golden man	Pg 52
14	The shining star	Pg 61
15	Phineus	Pg 63
16	The guests arrive	Pg 70
17	D Day minus one	Pg 72

18	Waiting for dawn	Pg 73
19	The calm before…	Pg 79
20	The dark tide	Pg 83
21	The courage of Sweetbriar	Pg 89
22	Cleon's charge	Pg 93
23	Breaking through	Pg 94
24	The line falters	Pg 97
25	Spartan's choice	Pg 99
26	Sacrifice	Pg 102
27	The grey company	Pg 109
28	Standing to	Pg 114
29	The price of victory	Pg 116
30	Honour the fallen	Pg 121
31	The beginning	Pg 127
32	Legacy of man	Pg 145
33	Appendices of Sweetbriar	Pg 156
34	Epilogue	Pg 160
35	About the author	Pg 161

1: PROLOGUE

The puppy lay comfortably at the end of the sofa. His blanket had been draped there and it was warm and snuggly. There was no sound to disturb him other than the ticking of the mantel clock. He glanced up at it. He knew time had passed with the passage of those slow-moving hands but as to the markings they pointed to, they meant nothing to a dog. How long had his beloved mistress been gone, it didn't matter, if she walked through the door one minute after leaving, he would get as excited as if she'd been gone for a week.

Suddenly his ears pricked up, someone was approaching the house. He leapt from the sofa and hurtled across the room to the open doorway. Mummy is home, he excitedly thought to himself, his tail wagging with glee. Through the doorway he bounded and along the hall. He could see the silhouette of her at the frosted glass window set into the front door. Then the sound of the key being inserted in the lock. It turned and slowly the door opened. Oh how exciting, his tail wagged even harder. There in the doorway she stood before him, but as he looked up at her face he froze, his tail no longer wagged.

They both stood in complete silence, the puppy staring at the place where her face should be. There was nothing, her face was blank, devoid of all features. No eyes, no ears, no mouth. Her head was as smooth and featureless as an egg. And then, as he stared up at her she began to fade as if turning into mist. She faded out of existence and was gone, only the door itself remained but that too was fading. Slowly around him the puppy saw the walls of his lovely home turn to nothing, as if none of it had ever existed at all. His place on the sofa vanished before him. The fireplace and mantel above it were gone, even the clock disappeared, though the steady ticking sound remained. And when at last he found himself alone in an empty void, with nothing to share it with but the sound of that invisible clock, he too began to fade, until finally, he was no more.

2: THE KEY TO GREENVALE

Young Rose sat atop the great mound enjoying the morning sunshine. It was tall and covered in tussocks of long grass but at its base and all around was a field of poppies swaying gently in the breeze. That great green mound rose like an island from an ocean of red waves. It is said that long ago there was a mighty battle fought here, though looking out at such serene beauty you wouldn't know it now. In fact, that area of swaying poppies was known as the field of valour and the mound upon which she sat was called victory hill, though it is more commonly nicknamed Cleon's throne for reasons unknown. Regardless of the myths, it had always been her favorite place to sit this time of year when all was in colour and bloom. But today was different, the time had come for her to set aside her childhood for she was almost grown up and today would be her first foray into the world of adulthood. She felt both excited and nervous for the day ahead. This was to be her first day at work, assuming of course the curator at the museum accepts her as his new apprentice. Her uncle had been the archivist there for many years, as had many more of her distant family before him. But his eyesight was not as it used to be, so he was hoping to find a replacement, and had recommended Rose on account of her keen interest in history and her inquisitive mind. She had the makings of an ideal historian he'd always said, and she did not wish to disappoint him. Suddenly her thoughts of the day ahead were interrupted.

"Rose, get down from there at once." came a voice from below, and looking down, Rose saw her mother approaching through the high poppies that surrounded her. With a slight sigh, Rose did as requested and walked down the bank towards her.

"I know mum, we've all heard the saying, **None may sit on Cleon's throne but Cleon himself.** Who was Cleon anyway?"

"I don't rightly know, but I assume he was some ancient king." Rose's mother replied as she reached her.

"Well, he must've been a great king to have such a large throne."

"I really couldn't say, you'd have to ask your uncle, he's more knowledgeable about such things than I, and speaking of your uncle, you need to get going, you don't want to be late on your first day. Run along now."

"Oh, is it time already?" And with that she scurried off towards the museum. "Love you mum, I'll see you later." she called back as she went.

Arriving before the entrance, she paused for a moment, not only to catch her breath, but also apprehensive about what awaited her beyond that seemingly cavernous doorway. It loomed high above her, its doorframe etched with a multitude of intricate carvings, the meaning of which was lost on her, but she assumed they somehow represented the historical relics stored within. This frame was crowned with a larger symbol comprised of a cross overlayed with two crescents placed back-to-back. To Rose it seemed to stare down at her like some divine eye, and she felt uncomfortable. But here she was, on the threshold of a possible new career. She set aside her nerves and entered.

The room inside was huge, its ceiling high above her, and all about were rows upon rows of artifacts. Carefully lined up for all to see were many different items of antiquity. Strange curiosities from a forgotten past, their former purpose in many cases now unknown. Amongst them she could see her uncle carefully cleaning one of the pieces.

"Hello Rose, you made it, welcome to the museum of history" he said with a smile as he spotted her "I hope you're ready for your first day, the curator is looking forward to meeting you."

"I am." she replied confidently, but her uncle could tell by the way her tail swished that she was feeling nervous. No matter what a squirrel may say, the instinctive movement of their tails always conveys their true emotions.

"Don't fret my dear, I'm sure you'll do just fine. The curator should be out in a moment, he's just popped into the back room to finish off some work."

While they waited, Rose looked closely at the item her uncle had been cleaning. It was a black rectangular shaped flattish object with a completely smooth face on one side. This smoothness was damaged by a crack that ran across one corner. On its side there appeared to be a couple of small, raised points that may have once been buttons though for what function they served there was no clue.

"What is it Uncle Burdock?" she enquired, confused by its strange shape and seemingly pointless purpose.

"To be quite honest I haven't got the slightest idea but judging by the large number we have unearthed over the years, and always in areas of former human settlement, clearly, they valued them greatly. Whatever purpose they once served is lost to us, but the humans it would seem could not go anywhere without one."

"Hello, I'm guessing you must be Rose, I'm Juniper", came a voice from the back of the room. Rose turned to see a kindly looking mole blinking at her.

"Hello Juniper, pleased to meet you," Rose replied shyly "I was just admiring your exhibits."

"Ah, the mysterious tablets" he replied seeing what they were looking at. "Some of the dogs believe they were some form of human communication device, but since we've never managed to get one to do anything at all, that remains purely theoretical. But speaking of exhibits, please follow me, I would like to show you something that we do at least understand."

Juniper led Rose towards the back of the room where there was a large piece of wood leaning against the wall, and piled around its base were many smaller, slender pieces of assorted size and length.

"Here we are," Juniper announced, "What do you make of this? Consider understanding this puzzling pile your job interview, now tell me what you see."

Rose stepped closer and examined the piece of wood leaning against the wall. It was quite large and rectangular but also quite thin, its surface was smooth except for some symbols scratched upon it. It was clearly no branch or log she had ever seen. As for the symbols, at the centre of them was scratched a picture of a tree, upon the top of which sat a raven. Around this ran an ornately carved circle, and overlayed upon this were five other symbols placed evenly around its circumference. One appeared to be a leaf of some kind; another was clearly an acorn. The others looked to be of a wolf, a cat and a dog. It seemed to her that these markings bore a resemblance, in style at least, to the symbols displayed around the frame of the museum entrance as if carved by the same paw.

Next, she turned her attention to the multitude of branches and sticks that were heaped at the base of this ornate panel. Each was also covered in many symbols, some she recognized, others she didn't. Rose considered herself a good reader, but the pictographs she had grown up learning did not use all the same symbols as these before her. It was as if she was trying to read a different language.

Each of the pieces of wood began most prominently with one of the symbols displayed on the larger carving. It seemed to her that the larger picture she had first inspected was somehow a guide telling her which pieces she needed to read. Reaching for one of the lengths, she thought she would try reading it, a short one should be simple enough. It began with a carving of the acorn, after which many other symbols continued along its length.

"What does it tell you?" Juniper enquired with interest.

"Well, I struggle to identify many of these symbols, but I can read enough to understand it tells something about a shiny star made from some kind of unusual metal. Is this some form of foreign language, for these writings are only vaguely similar to the pictographs I know?"

"Not foreign, original. These are the first known writings, the first words ever put to wood by your great ancestor, Sweetbriar herself. You no doubt already know she was the inventor of our written word, which has evolved over time to become the fully fleshed out pictographs we know today."

"Sweetbriar? Yes, she was a very distant relative of mine. Family legend tells that she was a wise elder squirrel from the early days of our community, but I did not know she was responsible for the creation of writing."

"Indeed she was, and much more besides, now please, try

another."

This time Rose selected one of the longer lengths, this one beginning with the wolf. Carefully her eyes followed the line of pictures making what sense of it she could.

"It seems to be telling something about a great battle, but it's not just about wolves. It includes all sorts, badgers, dogs, wolves and cats. It even involves squirrels and hedgehogs. There is danger and suffering mentioned here, but it also has hope and friendship. Clearly it tells of great deeds, but the exact details are lost on me."

"Very well done, I can see why your uncle has such high hopes for you, now let me explain what it all means."

Juniper moved closer to the larger symbol and began.

"Many remember Sweetbriar from history lessons as a kindly old squirrel, but few remember she too was young once, much as you are today. In her youth she had seen and experienced many great events, and it was her desire to ensure such stories would not be lost that inspired her to develop the writings she did in later life. The trouble was, for so long all we had was a pile of sticks with each telling a short story, but seemingly unconnected to one another in any apparent way. However, what we actually have here is the story of Greenvale, it's first written history. There are older histories of course but they were always handed down by word of mouth from one generation to the next, and survived to some degree only in the telling. These verbal stories were vulnerable to gradual embellishment over time, but this was the first to be written. This large carving for many years adorned the wall of one of the chambers in Frosthome Hall, and for all that time it was assumed to be simply a decorative panel. But after it was moved out to allow for refurbishment work at the hall, I got to examine it more closely and realised it is actually the key to unlocking those stories she had written. It shows which pieces of wood are required to tell the tale, each beginning with one of the chapter symbols displayed on the key. The wolf, cat and dog are easy enough to understand. So too is the Acorn for that has always been the symbol for Greenvale and all its inhabitants. And as for the leaf? Well, that is actually a

The Key to Greenvale

Shamrock and for the purpose of Sweetbriar's writings it represents the soldier, a character of great importance to the tale she has to tell."

"What is a soldier?" Rose enquired for she had never heard the word before.

"It was a human term for a member of their armies long ago. From what I understand, back in the olden days when humans walked the earth, if ever they went to war, it was their soldiers that did the fighting."

"So there was a human still living in Sweetbriars time, how is that possible?"

"Patience young Rose, only when Sweetbriar's tale is told will you have the answers you seek. And so, having selected only the sticks that bore these symbols I was able to assemble the story as she wished it to be told."

"But there are far more pieces here than the few symbols on the key, and the same symbols are repeated on many of them." Rose interrupted.

"Well spotted, and indeed you are correct. You see Sweetbriar was inventing writing as she went along and wasn't sure how best to structure her tales. Many chapters seem to be dependent on the length of wood available as much as their content, so even once I had sorted which pieces are relevant, we still have a seemly jumbled collection of sticks. These will only tell the story if assembled in the correct order, but unfortunately the key doesn't specify what that order is. However, I believe that after much work I have achieved exactly that."

"But how could you do that if you do not understand all the words, let alone the order in which they are read, where would you even begin?" Rose asked.

"Ah, but I do understand the words, I have dedicated many years to studying them. Though I must admit I added a little touch of my own by giving the chapters titles based on what they contain, artistic licence I call it. And as for where to begin, look again at the key and you tell me."

Once again Rose examined the key closely. It can't be any of those five symbols around the edge for she had seen them repeated on many of the branches and sticks. The tree in the centre she knew meant the end, for it is still a commonly used pictograph in the language of today. The fully grown tree represents fulfilment, completion, and signifies the end. So that leaves only that small raven sitting at its top. She pointed to it.

"There, that's where the story begins." She announced confidently.

3: A BIRD'S EYE VIEW

The raven woke to the morning sunrise, and looked out across the treetops at the high slopes of the valley walls rising up from the great expanse of brown leafed woodland that surrounded him, for it was Autumn and the leaves would soon fall. From his perch in the uppermost branches, he could see for many miles. Looking eastwards down to where the trees were older and more established but gradually thinned and gave way to a more grassy valley floor interspersed with patches of gorse and criss-crossed with the remains of old stone walls, and running down the centre of this valley he could see the scar of what may once have been a small road or track. The valley itself was formed between two spurs that ran eastwards from a great peak that loomed above the treetops behind him. These spurs gradually sloped downwards the further they extended until the valley itself merged into the gently rolling plain beyond. He had rested here during the night and would continue on his way shortly, but just as he was about to take flight something caught his attention. Down below on the forest floor he could hear voices. Being careful to remain hidden he hopped down a couple of branches for a closer look.

Below, on the bank of the sloping ground not far from the base of the tree he was in, he saw a small group of badgers. Nothing unusual in itself until he realised they were not talking to each other but to a mole and two young squirrels that accompanied them. The mole seemed to be giving the badgers directions to a point on the bank where some mole hills could be seen. Once satisfied with their instructions the badgers set to work excavating the site while the mole supervised, and the squirrels watched on with interest. What manner of place is this where badgers, moles and squirrels work together as friends the raven thought.

For several hours the badgers toiled, heaving both soil and stone from the bank, and all the while the raven watched, fascinated by this feverish activity. Then finally the work was done and where once a few mole hills had been, now a huge tunnel followed their route into the darkness, and into this passage the whole party went, their voices fading as they headed ever deeper until nothing more could be heard.

The raven pondered what he had seen then looked up at the sun. It was well past midday, and he should've been on his way hours ago, but this strange cooperation between completely different species baffled him. Badgers are ferocious creatures and would sooner eat a mole or a squirrel than take orders from one. As he mulled over what he had witnessed, he heard the voices returning, faint at first but getting louder as they neared the entrance to the passage. Eventually, they all emerged back into the sunlight and the raven listened intently as they continued their discussion amongst themselves. Of what they spoke he wasn't entirely sure, there was something about old ruins, something about a tunnel, presumably the one they had just dug, and also, mention of a locked door. Finally, with their conversation finished they parted ways, the mole and squirrels down the now enormous tunnel entrance and the badgers off into the woods. With the forest falling silent, the raven took stock of what he had seen and heard. A strange cooperation of different species working together, he mused, well that's a story to tell, but few would believe it. Birds are well known as the gossips of the world and ravens are presumably no different, so once he felt sure of it all in his head, he stretched his mighty wings and in a sweep of black he was away.

4: CLEON'S PRIDE

At the base of the rocky escarpment where the ground levelled off, many cats were seated in groups outside the entrance to a cave. Some injured from battle, many licking their wounds or simply resting uncomfortably in pain. The broken remnants of a defeated army. The vast majority were the small feral cats, descendants of former house cats that were, and still are found in large numbers across the land, a plentiful supply of disposable fodder for war, but amongst them were many of the larger wildcats that populate the northern wilderness. But even these were not the largest, for those were inside the cave. The privilege of size brought with it the privilege of rank. These were the chosen ones, chosen but not trusted, Cleon's inner circle. He kept them loyal by sowing the seeds of distrust between one another. They would never dare conspire against him since none could trust their fellow conspirators. And thus, each of them knew their only hope for advancement lay in proving their individual worth to Cleon himself, while eagerly betraying any infraction of the others.

They sat about in the cave, mostly separately, eying each other cautiously, a few of them were discussing matters together, but not as friends for friendship was unknown to them. And all the while a select few that made up Cleon's personal guard were ever watchful, their stern and silent gaze looking out for the slightest hint of dissent or treason. Into this cave walked a late arrival, a strong and ferocious wildcat fresh from a task he had been given by Cleon, and he had now returned to report the result. The prospect of doing so made him nervous, for Cleon does not take well to bad news and he was already enraged by his army's latest defeat. One of the guards ushered the wildcat forward, "Cleon awaits, you may proceed", he said with a nod to the back of the cave that was so shrouded in darkness only the vague shape of the giant leader could be discerned. The wildcat gulped and went forward.

From the shadows a deep voice growled, "Report, what did you find?"

The wildcat, with a dry mouth began his report.

"I returned to the field of battle as ordered sire. The wolves had already removed their fallen and had begun piling the bodies of our dead in heaps as is their tradition after a battle. I saw the black wolf himself overseeing them, he was accompanied by that accursed she-wolf carrying that dead puppy of hers they all seem so protective of."

"I care not for what the wolves were doing, what news of my son, did you find him?" Cleon hissed.

The wildcat reluctantly continued, "While the wolves were still at work in the lower end of the field I crept to the place where your son was last seen, and I regret to inform you that I found him dead as we feared."

In a flash, a great paw snatched out from the darkness and gripped the wildcat by the throat, "And what condition was his body, scarred from many wounds like the champion he was I trust."

Feeling the claws tighten around his throat the wildcat struggled an answer, "He was sire, a great many wounds for he fell in a blaze of glory", this was a lie, for Cleon's son was no hero. He had panicked in the battle and fled, but in his frenzied flight he had slipped and fell to his death over the edge of a ravine, the only marks upon him caused by the fall, and there his body remained unnoticed by the victorious wolves. An insignificant end to an insignificant cat.

Cleon's grip tightened and his claws pierced the wildcat's skin, "My heroic son lies dead with many wounds, yet you stand before me with none. By rights I should kill you where you stand, but I shall give you one last chance at redemption. In the next battle we fight you shall be my vanguard. You shall proceed before the army and prove your worth. Others shall accompany you, not to lend support, but to ensure you do not shirk from your duty. You shall find yourself glory in battle, or death if you should falter." And with that the mighty paw thrust the wildcat aside with such force that he stumbled to the ground. Picking himself up, and with his neck bleeding he slinked back away from the wrath of Cleon. A lucky escape he thought as he hissed at some of the other cats that were gloating at his admonishment.

Cleon lent forward from the shadows, his piercing eyes freezing all the chosen ones with terror. He seethed at them "All of you have failed me, your cowardice and weakness cost me my victory, and my son. I shall raise a new army far larger than before, and each and every one of you will prove your loyalty to me in battle. The next time we cross that pack of wolves, It will be their carcasses piled high for the sport of crows as they have done with ours".

When Cleon speaks all listen and when he orders they obey. They all knew their place in his society of one, he rules, they are ruled. Cleon was no ordinary wildcat; he was exceptional for two reasons. First, he had a name, the only wildcat to possess one, and second, he was far larger than any of the others for he was not a true wildcat, but a monstrous perversion of a fated union between a cougar and a wildcat, for Cleon's ancestor, also called Cleon, had escaped from Edinburgh Zoo back at the time of the great collapse and managed to find a mate and survive in the harsh cold conditions of Scotland. Since that time, the eldest surviving son of that line has assumed the name of Cleon on accession in honour of their great ancestor. Officially this Cleon was the 14th, and had his son lived, in time he should've taken on the mantle of Cleon the 15th. It was not too late in life for Cleon to sire a new son, but to do so would distract him from his desire for vengeance. If he was to destroy that black wolf and his pack, he needed to rally what forces he had left here, and then go in search of more. He would scour the land for all the wildcats and ferals he could round up, press gang them into service and return with the largest army the world has ever seen. Any that dare oppose him shall be crushed. This Cleon was unlike any of those that went before, for they were content only with commanding a powerful pride. This Cleon was ambitious and dreamt of much more, an empire with himself at its head, not as a mere Cleon the 14th, numbers were beneath him, but as Emperor Cleon the Mighty. So ambitious was he in fact that he had murdered his older brother to secure his place in the line of succession. An act his father viewed favourably as he described it at the time as, "An act of cruelty worthy of the name Cleon". His approval was short lived however, for he underestimated his second son's craving for power, and he too was to be murdered shortly afterwards. Now Cleon was free to pursue his ambition to the full. He would rule the world from his throne, and all would kneel before him, but only after his enemies are vanquished, and first and foremost amongst them were those accursed wolves.

5: FAREWELL SALUTE

Seamus led his team out of the HQ building into the crisp cold air. The morning sun was trying its best to shine through the thick grey clouds that had dominated the sky for so long now that few could remember their last sight of blue. It was still the tail end of winter, but spring should be fast approaching, and perhaps clear skies would accompany it. He glanced over at the vehicles that were parked nearby, the very vehicles that had brought them to this place. But their engines were cold for the fuel had been exhausted long ago. Now they stood as obsolete relics that would serve better purpose lining the halls of the Imperial War Museum.

He looked with sorrow out across the former lawn near the medical centre and cast his mind back to happier times when the soft grass served as a resting place for off duty soldiers to laze away the time reading books and magazines while the handlers from the guardroom exercised their guard and sniffer dogs. Now, by stark contrast it was a forlorn area pock marked with a multitude of mounds, the final resting place for so many of his fellow guardsmen. He could see a small burial party hard at work digging into the frozen ground. Then, from the medical centre door, came a stretcher party, their precious cargo bound for the cold embrace of the freshly dug soil. It seemed like a lifetime ago that the company was first sent to garrison this outpost in the back of beyond. Now that renowned company was so heavily reduced in numbers, they could barely muster a single platoon.

A little further along the road that led down to the main gate, a small detachment of sick but able-bodied soldiers formed up in a single rank along the kerb side. Seamus knew with such depleted numbers this garrison would soon fall but he had been denied the honour of falling by their side. His duty lay elsewhere. He swallowed hard for he knew the vital importance of the mission to which he and his team had been assigned.

He led his team forward, towards the line of awaiting

guardsmen. As they came level with them the sergeant brought the line to a salute, and they did so in perfect unison. A poignant reminder of those magnificent parades the regiment had performed with such precision in better times. He carried on past the saluting soldiers, he knew each and every one of them for they were all brothers of the colours, and they had served together for many years.

They continued down toward the gate where a single sentry waited. As they approached, the sentry drew the bolt and walked the gate open. Seamus and his companions stopped briefly. They looked silently at each other, reassuring themselves of the importance of their mission. They knew the honour of the regiment now rested with them and the fulfilment of their final orders, but they were saddened by the thought that they would never see their beloved comrades again. The threshold of this garrison formed the line of destiny they were about to cross. They didn't dare look back for they feared if they were to do so they would not be able to bring themselves to leave. But leave they must for every one of them knew their duty and so they set aside their emotions as best they could and marched on. Out through the open gateway that small detachment marched, never to return to this place of death.

6: THE COMPANY OF WOLVES

The great wolf sat motionless on the ridge, his eyes fixed on the distant eastern horizon. Brasidas was an enormous beast, his rough black coat stained by many seasons in the wild. Across his left eye ran a scar from a claw strike that had narrowly missed blinding him. A painful reminder of his last battle against Cleon the wildcat and his pride. It troubled him that Cleon had escaped that day, slinking off to lick his wounds in some damp forgotten hole. Brasidas knew the world had not seen the last of Cleon, and he would someday return to resume his vile ambitions for conquest. That had been just one of the many battles his company of wolves had engaged in over the years. They enjoyed a great advantage over their enemies thanks to the way they organized themselves for war, a pack structure developed and refined by successive leaders over the years. Brasidas currently commanded the company, with Darius, a highly competent and skilled leader in his own right, serving as second in command. The company itself was divided into three packs, each commanded by a seasoned and distinguished veteran, and these packs were further divided into teams, the strength and number of these could vary dependent on available numbers at the time. And each of these teams were led by young but competent potential future leaders chosen for their initiative and leadership skills more than fighting prowess. And behind all this was the rearguard composed of those either too young or too old for combat but an essential part of family life for the company. It was into this rearguard that the oldest veterans would retire but continue to serve as instructors and trainers for the young pups that would eventually take their place in the company. They had developed a simple order system that allowed commands to be barked quickly and efficiently down the chain ensuring each and every set of paws on the ground knew exactly what was required of them at any given moment. This structured yet simple system had proven its value countless times against the mob tactics of the wild forces they had encountered despite often being heavily outnumbered.

But this year, Brasidas hoped for something other than war. He awaited the first rays of the morning sun, as he had done every morning for the last two weeks. Winter would soon be turning to spring and the hunting season could soon resume.

Below in the frost covered glen his great company of warriors waited patiently for his order. For just as he had ascended the ridge every morning, they had eagerly assembled ready to move should he command them to do so. For all creatures, winter is a time to take shelter and hunker down, but for these fearsome beasts born for the thrill of the hunt and forged in the field of battle there is no greater misery than idleness.

Briefly, Brasidas shifted his gaze over to the northern end of the glen. There in the dim half-light below a snowcapped mountain he could just make out the rugged outcrops of broken walls. A ruined city from the past, now nothing but a shattered reminder of a long-forgotten world. It's glassless windows now just black holes through which the wind echoes on a stormy night like the mournful howls of a grieving widow. He tried to imagine its former inhabitants, but all his mind could conjure were ghosts. Grey faceless shapes drifting through the ruins, for no human had been seen on this earth for over a hundred years and no living thing today is exactly sure what they looked like. Only a vague idea of their size and shape could be gleaned from the bones and relics they left behind, and the descriptions passed down through the generations. For all their achievements, for all their hopes and dreams, all that remained of mankind now were the fading scars of their crumbling ruins. With that, he snapped his mind back to the present. He turned his eyes back eastwards. What went before matters not, he told himself, now there is only the hunt. Brasidas was first and foremost a hunter. He lived for the hunt, and he commanded a mighty hunting party. His personal obsession with humans was an unnecessary distraction.

Slowly there formed a pale glow in the sky. Soon the sun would crest the horizon, and a new day would begin. The great wolfs' eyes were transfixed on that glimmer of light yet behind his eyes there was a concern, would this be the day they have been so desperately waiting for, or must they stay longer in this cold forsaken place. And if this is the day to move, where will it lead.

He cast his mind back to all the previous campaigns, the endless years of hunting he had been fated to lead. But for all the company's great deeds, distances covered, and obstacles overcome, the ultimate prize had always eluded him, as it had done for all the company commanders that went before. However, this year may be different for word had come to him of a wooded valley far to the south. An interesting place he'd heard, where animals live together in peace. Prime hunting ground that could contain the greatest prize of all time. He pondered this possibility, maybe this year his great hunt will finally end. He still possessed great strength, but he knew his age was overtaking him and he would soon be taking his place in the rearguard. Darius was more than ready to assume command and if this was to be his final hunt then let it be triumphant.

Suddenly his eyes lit as the first ray of sunlight crested the distant horizon. He lifted his head to the heavens and sniffed the air keenly. For wolves, their greatest sense is that of smell, and if spring was coming, he would know it. But there was nothing. He lowered his head, frustrated that this morning was not the one. He looked down at his company, knowing their disappointment that his news would bring, but just as he stood up to begin the walk back down the slope, there was a slight change in the breeze. Barely detectable to most, but Brasidas was not most. He froze in his tracks, looked about to where the breeze had come and inhaled deeply.

With this he was rejuvenated, all doubt passed from his mind, and he bolted down the slope towards the waiting wolves. "We move" he barked as he thundered through them, and a mighty howl erupted. The host gathered as one great mass and with their leader at the fore they hurtled southwards down the glen.

7: NEIGHBOURS

It was late March in Greenvale and Spring had finally established itself, and the forest was alive with the buzz of activity. Sweetbriar and Bramble sat near the tunnel entrance examining the curious artifacts laid out before them. They were a pair of young grey squirrels, Sweetbriar being the oldest and Bramble was her younger brother. Although not yet fully grown they considered themselves mature enough to work, and work they did. Not the normal everyday toil of other squirrels such as gathering and storing nuts, no, these two were helping Elderberry their mole friend with his archaeology project. Elderberry fancied himself as something of an amateur historian, his frequent tunnelling had unearthed many interesting finds, and he was determined to use them to help him piece together the long-forgotten past. Of course, while Elderberry was good at tunnelling, his paws were ill suited to the delicate manipulation of the items he discovered, so that's where Sweetbriar and Bramble came in. Their dexterous paws, like tiny hands, were nimble enough to examine the workings of some of the most intricate of pieces that came to light. The latest collection of which was laid out before them.

The first item was very strange, it consisted of a pair of connected frames made of some unknown black material and within these frames were set some form of hard material without colour or hue through which Sweetbriar could see. One of these transparent panes was cracked but still it remained fixed inside its frame. On each side of this object were hooked arms that had apparently at some stage hinged, though the mechanism was now so rusted in the open position that attempting to close them would probably break them. As for what this was for, she couldn't even guess.

Next Sweetbriar picked a perfectly spherical and smooth item about the size of her head, and examined it closely. It was blue and made of some strange material that was not hard like stone but had a bit of give to it if squeezed. It wasn't heavy so she assumed it was hollow. She turned it about in her paws but could find no discernible purpose to this curious object. Finally, baffled by what it was, she dropped it back into the pile and moved on to the next item.

Bramble sat next to her, and he too was curious about this object, so picking it up he began sniffing it. It smelt of earth for it had only recently been dug up by Elderberry. As he did so, unseen eyes were watching him intently from the nearby undergrowth. Bramble's curiosity was beginning to wane, he wanted to go play in the trees but wasn't allowed to go off on his own. With a bored sigh he threw the object as far as his little paws would allow. Suddenly, in a flash, something rushed from the bushes to intercept the object. Sweetbriar and Bramble were startled and fell backwards with surprise. There in front of them, bouncing and bounding about was a dog. The squirrels had heard of such creatures for they lived in another valley some miles to the south of their own, but neither Sweetbriar nor Bramble had ever seen one. This one though, they could tell was clearly not a fully grown adult dog but a puppy, although older and much larger than themselves. Because dogs live longer overall, their puppies don't mature until much later in life than the fast childhood of squirrels. It grabbed the object in its mouth and immediately brought it back towards Bramble. Dropping it in front of him, it then spoke in a broken immature way, "Throw ball again, throw ball, play with Trixie, please".

"Ball?" Bramble enquired.

"Yes ball, throw ball again".

Bramble threw the ball again and Trixie ran off to retrieve it.

"Looks like you've found a new play mate, Bramble." Sweetbriar said with a smile.

Again, Trixie brought the ball back and again Bramble threw it with all his might. This continued until they were abruptly interrupted.

"What's all this racket, can't a mole work in peace around here?" Said Elderberry as he poked his head out from the tunnel entrance. "And what on earth is that dog doing with my artifact?"

"That dog is named Trixie and the artifact is a ball, Trixie called it so." Sweetbriar replied, "It seems to be a toy from the old world, though how she would know, I can't say."

"Ah, that's a classic example of instinctual knowledge at work" Elderberry explained "Just like an orphaned squirrel without parents to teach it, would still know to forage and bury nuts for winter. But far more importantly, where did she come from and what's she doing here?"

"Trixie lost, want find home, friends help Trixie, please." She said, dropping the ball as she did so, then quickly retrieving it as it had clearly become precious to her.

Elderberry, thought for a moment before deciding. "We must take her to Lord Hawthorn, he will know what to do". And so, without further need for discussion, off the four went towards Frosthome Hall, the home of the badger lord and his kin.

When they arrived, Lord Hawthorn was seated on a bank outside the entrance to his hall, listening to a group of rabbits appealing for help in removing some tree roots that were hindering their planned warren extension project. When smaller animals need help with heavy work they often rely on the badgers for assistance. Badgers are renowned for their great strength and helpful nature, but they are too few in number to help everybody all at once, so aid must be prioritized. In this case, the priority tasks were focused on repairing any damage done by the high winds of winter. The enlargement of the rabbits' warren will be needed most next winter when all are hunkering down inside, but for now it was still spring, so the issue was not so pressing. Lord Hawthorn assured the rabbits that the works will be carried out in good time but for now it would need to wait.

With the rabbits satisfied with Lord Hawthorn's assurances, they hopped away. Now he saw the strange party that awaited an audience.

"Welcome Elderberry, judging by the presence your strange companion, I take it you have not come to request help with another one of your archaeology projects". He said with his eyes fixed on Trixie.

"No sire, Sweetbriar and Bramble have found this stray puppy in the woods and it needs to be guided home, but we do not know the way."

Hawthorn sighed before responding. "Of all the important tasks that need fulfilling around here, this could not have come at a worse time. However, returning this puppy to its home is of the utmost importance. We have had little involvement with our estranged neighbours over the years, and while there is no hostility between us, we cannot risk a diplomatic incident by failing to return this puppy of theirs. In fact, for some time now I have been pondering the notion of breaking the ice between our two societies, and perhaps this is the catalyst for us to do so".

"Hurrah!" cried Bramble, "We're taking you home Trixie, what an adventure we shall have."

"Oh no Bramble, this will be no trip for little ones, bringing this to my attention, your roll here is done. I shall take her myself" Hawthorn said sternly.

Trixie listened intently while trying to formulate the words, before speaking "Trixie go with Bramble, Bramble friend of Trixie"

The lord thought for a moment, "Alright, since it seems I cannot take one without the other, then so be it, but Sweetbriar will need to come too" he said turning to her, "You shall help me keep an eye on your little brother".

"And me." Interrupted Elderberry, "While their parents are away, Sweetbriar and Bramble are entrusted into my care remember, if they are going with you, I go too. Besides, these dogs seem to know stuff about the past that may help me in my studies".

"Well, it seems settled then. Not exactly the way I thought my day would pan out when I awoke this morning, but since arguing against you all will no doubt be futile, I guess we're all going. It'll be a long trek, easy going for Trixie and I, but perhaps too long for little legs, so I suggest Elderberry, Sweetbriar and Bramble ride on my back."

"Bramble on Trixie, please, Bramble my friend." Trixie chimed in excitedly.

And so, with bramble carrying the blue ball and seated on

Trixie's back, and Sweetbriar and Elderberry clambering onto Lord Hawthorn, off they set, up the wooded southern slope of the valley side, and beyond the crest of the ridge, many miles of rolling hills lay between Greenvale and the territory of the dogs.

8: THE FAITHFUL

Delphine and the other dogs in her small party had been searching all morning and it was now midday that the trail had led them to the very border of their territory. When little Trixie had got lost the day before, in her desperation to find her way home she had wandered this way and that, snaking her way through the forest with no apparent direction in mind. The search party had been following her scent and as such had been forced to spend much time weaving about also, but now the trail left their land, and they had halted briefly to be sure before continuing. Just as they were about to cross that unmarked boundary, they heard a noise from ahead, something was approaching.

Delphine, as the largest in the group, stood at the front, ready to respond to whatever this may be. She was a sandy brown dog similar in shape and build to what was once called a golden retriever, but she had a rougher, more wiry coat. No pure breeds existed anymore, the old pedigrees of the past had long been lost in the mix of time.

As she waited, she heard voices coming from a little way off in the woods. Whatever this was, she thought, it was not alone. Then, to her surprise, emerging from the bushes ahead she saw the strangest of sights. There was Trixie with a little squirrel on her back, and next to her walked an enormous and ferocious looking badger, and on his back sat another squirrel and a mole.

Whilst pleased and relieved to see Trixie safe and well, Delphine felt apprehensive of this badger. Not wishing to appear intimidated, in her most authoritative voice she could muster she called out to him. "Welcome to the lands of the faithful, stranger, it pleases us to see the safe return of our little one. To whom do I have the pleasure?"

In his usual bold manner Lord Hawthorn announced himself "I am Hawthorn, Lord of Frosthome Hall and guardian of Greenvale, and my companions here are Elderberry the mole, Sweetbriar the squirrel, and the smaller squirrel you see is her younger brother Bramble."

"An impressive title Hawthorn, Lord of Frosthome Hall" Delphine replied with a hint of sarcasm, "I am Delphine, just Delphine".

Lord Hawthorn felt a little embarrassed with himself, for it was the foolish pride of his wild ancestors that created the rift between the two societies in the first place. If he was to heal the old wounds, then he needed to be less arrogant than they had been. Even the title of lord was a hangover from the wild past when the senior male of each set was addressed by his kin as lord, and since Frosthome was the largest and most esteemed set in Greenvale, the other animals, both badger and non-badger alike, still addressed him as such. The trouble is, even now, badgers can be a bit full of themselves at times which makes them come across as boastful and pompous, but their hearts are in the right place. Not a good start, he thought.

As Lord Hawthorn was thinking this over, Delphine had concerns of her own. She had just spotted the blue ball that Bramble was holding and realised that if the little squirrel was to throw it, her instincts would immediately cut in and force her to chase it like the puppy that lurks inside all dogs regardless of age when there's a ball involved. How could she maintain her dignity in front of this badger lord if she's running after a ball with her tail wagging. She managed to suppress her concern and continued.

"I must confess I am a little surprised. I was under the impression you animals of the wild did not have names, and yet here you are presenting them."

"It is true our wild ancestors did not have names, but times have changed greatly since those dark days of the past. And speaking of our wild ancestors, it is a past wrong of theirs that I hope to finally address. With your permission my lady, may I meet with the leader of your community?"

"Our community is one of equality so does not have a leader as such, but we do have one of great age and wisdom that advises and guides us in time of need. Her name is Alice, and I will gladly take you before her for an audience."

So together the group set off through the trees with Delphine leading the way. Up a long slope they went until they crested an unseen ridge, covered in trees on both sides so it afforded no view of either the land forward or back, and then they began descending once more. It was for quite some time before they finally emerged from the trees into a more open area of rough tufty grassland not too dissimilar from the open area in Greenvale except this was dominated by a large lake. By its banks many dogs could be seen, some resting and some playing for there were many puppies of varying age and size here. Trixie spotted her parents and immediately bolted towards them, with little bramble still seated on her back.

"Don't worry, he'll be safe here, we dogs are very protective of little ones, it's in our nature." Delphine said to Sweetbriar reassuringly."

Delphine led them further along the side of the lake towards a great wooded area where they could see seated just before it a large group of adults gathered around a single large female who seemed to be addressing them about something. This must be Alice, Hawthorn thought, and sure enough he was correct. As they approached the dogs gave way to allow them to pass freely, though not without some element of caution for although few of them had ever encountered a badger before, they had all heard of their ferocity if provoked.

Delphine spoke first. "Alice, may I please present to you Lord Hawthorn from Greenvale, he wishes to address you."

Alice looked him up and down, a curious sight indeed with a mole and a squirrel still perched on his back. "We have for too long believed badgers to be somewhat arrogant, so it pleases me to see from the fact that you carry such passengers freely, that you do possess a level of humility after all, so please Lord Hawthorne, accept my apology for misjudging your kind so wrongly in the past."

Hawthorn bowed his head graciously before replying. "My Lady, you have no cause to apologise for it was no misjudgment on your part. My ancestors were indeed as arrogant as you believe, and it is for that reason that I come before you. It was the arrogance of the wild badgers that scorned you so badly when you first settled in this area all those long generations ago, and for that I am truly sorry. As the wild creatures they were back then, they considered themselves true wildlife, while they viewed your ancestors that first came as not true wild animals but rather unwelcome trespassers from the world outside. Rather than helping you to learn the ways of the wild, they chose instead to ostracize you, and treat you with disdain. A fatal mistake on their part as it turned out, for when the great catastrophe came in earnest and the winters grew far more perilous than ever before, their refusal to cooperate with creatures other than themselves was to prove their downfall. Only by swallowing their pride and working together with others could badgers hope to survive, but few of them were prepared to do so. That is why there are so few of us today. Though our numbers are slowly returning, it will take time, for the damage to our population during those dark times was great, and those that are here today can freely admit that it was the compassion of a humble squirrel that saved us from our self-destructive nature and made us all the better for it. And as this better badger that stands before you, please accept my most humble and sincere apology to yourself and all your kind, past, present, and future."

Alice smiled kindly "How could I, or any other refuse to accept such an eloquent apology, my good Lord, but please, there was one part of it that intrigues me. You mentioned owing your salvation to a squirrel, please be so kind as to elaborate."

"Whilst that story is of great importance to us badgers, it is not rightly our story to tell, so please, if I may, hand over the telling of this tale to young Sweetbriar here."

Jumping down from his back and then helping Elderberry down behind her, Sweetbriar stood nervously before Alice. She knew the story of course, all squirrels did, but never had she been asked to tell it before so many, let alone on such an important occasion as this. The gathering of dogs around her, attentively waiting for her to speak, she gulped and began.

9: FROM TINY ACORNS GROW…

In the dark past of distant years when the great catastrophe came, none were prepared for the wrath of nature that was to be unleashed upon the world. The animals of the land had gone about their business mostly oblivious of one another, let alone the world outside. Human activity was simply something to be avoided. As the sights and sounds of man gradually diminished, at first it seemed like a blessing. No longer were friends and family dying under the wheels of the human machines that sped through the hard lanes that cris crossed our country. But those blessings were short lived for they were soon replaced by a new peril. The seasons we knew and lived our lives by were slowly merging from four to only two. A burning hot summer of drought and shortage, followed by freezing winters of storms, starvation and death. As the conditions worsened with each passing year, fewer and fewer of the animals would emerge to see the next brutal summer.

With the changing conditions, many of the plants and trees we relied on for food withered and died, never to return. And with the loss of habitat many species also vanished from the world, even bees have not been sighted in a hundred years. And all this time our wild ancestors continued to live apart, trying to survive as best they could in an environment that was far different from the one they had evolved for over countless millennia.

Then one year, during one of the harshest of winters, all that was about to change. For one of my ancestors who would later become named Acorn, was to set the fate of all the creatures of the wild on a new course. A course that ultimately led to the close community we have become.

He, like all squirrels was equally vulnerable to the harsh winters, for although squirrels are experts at foraging for and storing food, their dreys are not so sturdy against the high winds that ripped through the land so frequently. Many were destroyed in those storms, their occupants falling to their deaths as they slept. And even if their drey was not ripped from the trees by wind, the freezing temperatures were still bad enough to kill many.

But one morning after one such storm in which Acorn's drey was fortunate enough to survive, he looked down at the forest floor below and saw a weak and emaciated badger crawling from her set in search of food. The normal diet of badgers is earthworms but in this frozen ground the worms have gone too deep and are in very short supply, so her only hope was to find an alternative. Sadly, she lacked the strength for this herculean task, for she was too starving to muster the energy required, and after some futile attempts at crawling ever forward, she laid her head down to rest and passed into a deep sleep from which she never awoke. Acorn knew this was the fate that awaited many of the creatures around him, and as for his own family, while not starving, for he had stockpiled more than enough for them to eat, death could strike them at any moment in this bleak and violent climate they now lived. Then an idea struck him, with this badger now dead, here was an empty set. While it has never been in a squirrel's nature to live below ground, it was certainly a warmer and safer place to be than at the top of a tree in a storm. And so, leaving his family asleep for the moment, down the tree he clambered to investigate this potential new home.

At the entrance he paused, there was of course the scent of badger, but no sound from inside could he hear. Cautiously he crept into the darkness. Acorn's eyes were ill suited to darkness but gradually they adjusted enough for him to make out that he found himself in a huge chamber. An ideal home this would make, he thought. Plenty of room for not only his whole family to hunker down and see out the winter, but he could also move his stockpile of nuts and acorns in here also. Safe and secure from the harsh elements outside. He scurried back to his drey and set about the task of relocating his family to this new sanctuary.

It took many trips to bring all the supplies but finally it was done. So much of it needed moving in fact, that they were all exhausted from the exertion, and so they nestled down to sleep in this new safe haven. That first night was broken in the early hours when Acorn awoke to a strange sound coming from further in the darkness at the back of the chamber. It was like a faint whimpering noise and was coming from a back passage he hadn't initially noticed when he first entered the set. It seems his new home was far larger than he first realised, and worryingly, it seemed something else was in residence. Doing his best to suppress his fear, he edged slowly down the passage feeling the sides as he went so as not to lose his way. Finally, the passage opened into another large chamber, though smaller than the first, and it was here that he found them. Laying on the floor of the room, huddled together for warmth were four badger cubs. Weak and half-starved, they were whimpering as if calling for their mother who Acorn knew would not return. In the absence of worms badgers would eat anything, including squirrels if they could catch one. Acorn knew this and his first thought was to flee, but then something happened inside him, he felt pity. How could he abandon these innocents to the slow painful death of starvation. He scurried back to his stores and scooped up as many acorns as he could carry before rushing back to those poor trembling orphans. As soon as they smelt the acorns, they knew they could eat them and eat they did, as fast as their little mouths would allow. So fast in fact that Acorn needed to rush back for more. Several trips were needed before they finally felt content and went to sleep with full bellies and happy smiles. Acorn returned to his family in the larger chamber and slept as well, though this time with a nagging concern. Were his family safe from these badger cubs, what if they wake from their sleep and crave something larger than acorns. Had he done the right thing, he pondered.

The next morning he awoke to find he and his family were all perfectly safe. Was it all a dream, he asked himself. Rising, he crept back down the passage and sure enough there were the cubs fast asleep. As he approached, one of them woke, which in turn led the others to yawn and open their eyes also. They looked eager for more food so he returned to get some, but this time they followed him. Bringing baby badgers back to his family may be a surprise for them but what else could he do, so he resigned himself to the fact that his family has just got a lot larger. He needn't have worried though, it turned out the cubs and his own kits bonded instantly. So there they all were, braving the winter together as one giant extended family. The days turned to weeks, the weeks to months, and all of them were nourished by the stockpiled supplies, and the warmth of each other in this sheltered subterranean home. Finally, the harshness of the winter began to soften, and it was time to venture outside.

The first few weeks of better weather were mostly spent foraging for whatever could be found. As the ground thawed, more worms could be found near the surface and the badger cubs, already healthy and strong, grew even larger as they feasted on this new source of food. All was well with the family, and they thrived together as one, but then, in the fullness of time trouble was to find them, for nothing stays secret for long in a world watched by birds. Their gossip had reached the ears of the badger lords who sent a messenger to summon the four young badgers to a moot. It was the custom of the badger lords to hold an assembly they called a moot when serious matters must be addressed, and there was nothing more serious and shameful in the eyes of the lords than badgers mixing freely with non-badgers.

As the four badgers made ready to depart with the messenger, Acorn refused to let them go without him, he considered himself after all their guardian. The messenger was not pleased with this, but Acorn would not be dissuaded so off they went together. When they arrived at the moot, the badger lords were already assembled. Not so many as years passed for the climate had played a heavy toll on their numbers, and now only seven lords remained, and even these were not as large and well fed as those of earlier times. They were seated in a half circle with the largest at the centre and three each side of him in decreasing size and importance. It was the custom of the moot that the largest badger will assume the role of judge, and while not directly involved in the discussions, will cast the final verdict. Other badgers were gathered around to observe proceedings. The four cubs were ordered forward to stand in line before the moot, and much to the annoyance of the assembly Acorn joined them.

"Begone squirrel" one of the lesser lords barked, "This is badger business, and you have no place here".

Acorn held his ground, "These young cubs are in my care, so I have every right to be here", he insisted.

The badger lord looked furious "How dare you challenge my authority, I am a lord and my word is final. These cubs are here on trial, you are not, so begone".

"On trial for what?" Acorn replied

"Cohabitating with non-badgers, this is not the badger way and brings shame to us all". The lord growled, angrily.

Acorn snapped back without hesitation, "Then it is time to change the badger ways, while there's enough of you left to do so. Look at yourselves, sitting there half-starved and weakened by winter, you look more like wraiths than lords. And count yourselves, your diminished numbers do not lie. However, there is an alternative to this slow decline in all of us, but you must set aside your worthless pride to see it."

"Enough of this pesky squirrel" another lord interjected, "I want to hear from the accused, what do you have to say in your defence?" he demanded, looking at the four young badgers before him.

They looked at each other before one of them spoke, "We know nothing of the so called badger ways for we were orphaned as the smallest of cubs, we know only of the life we have lived, and from what we see from your wasted appearance, ours has proven the better."

This enraged the badger lords further, how can these young badgers dare to criticise the badger ways, such heresy was unheard of. But as they began to snarl and bicker with rage, the large lord that had until now remained silent suddenly interrupted "Enough!" he yelled, and the angry moot fell silent. While they had raised their questions, he had sat in silence observing the four strong and healthy badgers lined up before them, and noted the stark contrast against the rest of his kind.

"It is clear to me, that our way is failing, and here comes this squirrel claiming there is an alternative, we would be fools not to listen to whatever he has to offer, so please squirrel, let us hear what you are suggesting."

Acorn cleared his throat and began. "Both our kinds are suffering from these harsh winters that ravage the land with increasing ferocity each year, and as much as these four young badgers owe their survival to the supplies of acorns I was willing and able to share, my family is also in their debt. For it was their rightful home in which we found sanctuary from the storms, and so we thrived also. I propose that we form a union of all squirrels and badgers that we may winter together in peace and prosperity. That way we shall stand a greater chance of seeing the next summer, and many more to come. Divided we are all weaker than we can be combined. This should become the new way for both badger and squirrel alike".

The big lord thought for a moment before passing his judgement. "I have listened to your proposal, and I shall retire to deliberate, I hereby suspend this moot until tomorrow when I shall deliver my verdict. I shall send for you squirrel when the time is ready, so for now, you and your wards may return to your home."

"But how will I know which squirrel to fetch?" the badger messenger enquired. "All squirrels look alike to us".

The lord thought for a moment then replied, "This is true, and I'm sure we badgers look alike to squirrels also. Then we shall call him Acorn, and he shall answer to that name when summoned. Is that solution agreeable to you Acorn".

"It is sire, but if we are to use names to avoid confusion between the species, by what name shall I address you?"

"Hmm" the lord thought, "Since yours is the name of something that grows, then all names should be selected on that basis. I shall like something that is tall and strong, to remind me of my strength of earlier years when I was in my prime."

"How about Lord Oak?" Acorn suggested, "The oak tree is the tallest and strongest thing that grows I can think of".

"It is a strong word, but a bit short. I was hoping for something a bit more impressive sounding".

"Then I have it, Lord Blackthorn. The fruit of the blackthorn is dark to represent your coat, while its flowers are as white as the stripes on your head".

"Now that is an impressive name, Lord Blackthorn." the lord said with a smile.

And so it was that Acorn became the first wild animal to adopt a name, and Lord Blackthorn became the second. And the tradition of naming themselves after the things that grow in the wild has remained the custom ever since.

With the moot now suspended they all retired to their respective homes to await the dawn and the next assembly. When the messenger arrived and summoned Acorn and the four badgers, the call also included Acorn's entire family. This was not expected but they dutifully followed as requested. This strange development seemed all the more peculiar when they arrived at the moot and found that all the animals of the valley had been summoned. They were many and varied, not just badgers and squirrels but hedgehogs, mice, moles, rabbits and hares, even the foxes were there looking confused as to why. And at the centre of the moot sat Lord Blackthorn, waiting for the assembly to settle. Once satisfied the gathering was complete, he raised his paw for silence and delivered his verdict.

"No doubt many of you are wondering why you have been called to this moot. This squirrel that is now known as Acorn has proposed a union between badger and squirrel that I have spent the night deliberating upon, but my decision applies to far more than badgers and squirrels alone. Acorn's suggestion is a valid one, but I believe, for it to fully work it must go further. All our species are suffering in equal measure from the harshness of the world in which we now find ourselves, so my proclamation is thus. All the species of the valley shall become as one, working and living together in a single society that serves the betterment of all. I, and my fellow lords shall enlarge our sets to house all that wish to shelter there through the next winter. The squirrels shall oversee the collection and storing of supplies. None that wish a place in this community shall be turned away, and any that would seek to harm it shall be opposed by its duly appointed guardians, the badgers. And this notion of harm includes those animals that would normally feed on other members of this new society. No longer will they do so, acorns, nuts, fruits, insects, earthworms and roots shall become our only diet, so think carefully foxes if you wish to remain in this valley. This is my judgement and any that wish to ignore it and continue their lives alone are free to do so. I would caution against such a decision, but will not force my will upon you. And so, with my decision made and with the union between the squirrels and badgers already determined, I hereby declare this, the last ever badger moot to be concluded. From henceforth we shall hold shire moots, open to all members of our community."

With Lord Blackthorn's address over, the animals at first were stunned to silence. Never before had such a society been suggested to them, nor even imagined by them. But as the words sank in, they realised the wondrous future this proposal offered and began to feverishly chatter to one another, introducing themselves to each of the gathered species. A few of the more arrogant badger lords were unimpressed by what they considered to be a non-badger arrangement and left the assembly for their own homes. Their part in the story of the valley ended there for even if they and their families did survive the winters that followed, nothing is known of their fate.

But the community that formed thrived, and the largest of sets, that of Lord Blackthorn was enlarged still further and became known as Frosthome Hall for it was the winter home for many. The other animals began adopting names for ease of understanding and identifying one another, and over time, each species found they had a skill that could best serve more than just their own kind. It was the compassion of my ancestor Acorn that set us on a better course, and the wisdom of Lord Blackthorn that steered us to fruition. And although those years of harsh winters and burning summers are long behind us, and the four seasons have since returned to the world again, the unity we created for ourselves has endured. For none of us wish to return to the wild and lonely ways of our past, and so our story concludes as it spans the gap between who we were and who we are today.

With her story told, Sweetbriar looked around at the silent dogs. Silent because they loved every word of her tale, for dogs love to hear stories.

Lord Hawthorn smiled at her, "Very well told Sweetbriar, I could not have done the story justice myself."

Alice was impressed and responded, "That truly was an amazing tale, and it shows our two communities have evolved along similar lines. Whilst our ancestors held great loyalty towards their former human families, they initially held no such loyalty towards one another. It was only through cooperation were they able to survive the harsh reality in which they found themselves, but even so, your ancestors were right to consider ours as trespassers from the outside world for that is precisely what they were, the dispossessed from the human world they had lived their lives in. Former pets, that found themselves without masters, forced to wander in search of a new home. But we always remember the happier times that our ancestors once enjoyed in their human households and kept alive in story form through the generations. The history of the world they knew and loved, and the lives they lived is as real to us as if we had lived those lives ourselves. And since that time, we have called ourselves The Faithful in honour of our ancestors' loyalty to their former human families. Even our naming system pays homage to those golden days. We continue to use a combination of the original pet names given to our ancestors by humans, or the names of those very humans themselves. Since you have so graciously shared your story with us, it is only fitting that you may hear ours if you wish it."

"It would be an honour to learn your history my lady" Lord Hawthorn replied courteously. And so, as they all listened attentively, Alice began.

10: THE FALL OF MAN

It is said that in the ancient earliest of times when primitive man first discovered fire, a group of them sat huddled before the flickering flames for warmth. From the darkness of the forest a cold and hungry dog gazed in wonder at these strange creatures and their unusual orange creation that danced merrily before them.

Gripped by curiosity, the dog edged closer, keeping to the shadows cast by this marvel he moved unseen but ever closer. As the distance reduced, he began to feel the emanating warmth and it felt too good to resist and he continued to approach. Drawn by its splendour he abandoned all caution and stepped forward into the circle of light. Suddenly the humans saw him but to his amazement rather than drive him away, they took pity on his bedraggled and cold appearance. They beckoned him to come closer and as he tentatively did so, they offered him a share of their meagre rations. There they sat warming themselves by the fire, eating what food they had as friends until at last with their bellies full and their bodies warm they went to sleep.

Humans were a very different creature to other animals. While we augment our limited vocabulary with a multitude of variations in tone and pitch, the humans, whose hearing is less finely attuned than ours were required to use a vast number of different words and sounds in order to communicate. While we can easily convey detailed and concise information through a few sounds of varying tone, to human ears it was simply the same repetitive noise. And likewise, their seemingly jumbled sentences composed of many different words and phrases was confusing gibberish to us. Yet despite this obvious flaw, there was something kindly about them that this dog perceived, and while he could not understand their language, nor could he utter it himself, he found safety and comfort in their company.

And this was not an isolated story, for wherever man and dog met the same bond was formed. All over the land humans grew to love their new companions they shared the world with, and over time, as the humans began to advance and build themselves more permanent shelters their canine companions joined them, the histories of dog and man became one.

For thousands of years mankind continued to advance their culture. Always learning, adapting, inventing and building. They formed factions and communities, lines were drawn on their maps and their languages and customs diverged. Sometimes they would wage war against each other, and other times form bonds of friendship, and always the dogs were by their side, bearing witness to events they barely understood. It always seems strange to us dogs how humans could have more love for us than they often did for each other.

The humans adapted themselves and their world. Huts were replaced by larger homes, camps became villages, then towns. Some settlements grew into cities. Scrub land gave way to cultivated farmland, and food became abundant. Man used horses for transport, as well as boats and ships. Then great iron rails were laid across the land and mighty engines belching steam thundered their way over huge distances. Then roads were laid and new machines of travel were free to go beyond the confines of narrow rails. Mighty flying machines carried people up into the clouds, and the dogs bore witness to it all.

Finally, when it seemed the lives of humankind had advanced their conditions to a life of comfort and leisure it all started to fail. What we now call the great catastrophe didn't come suddenly so it wasn't until too late they realized what was happening. Dogs listened with confusion while their human families argued about the weather. News stories flashed on the screens of the television's humans had in their homes. Images of floods and storms, men pointed at maps and talked seriously about heat and cold. Images of huge factories and power plants, their great chimneys belching black smoke. The dogs saw these images and heard these news stories and while they couldn't fully understand human words, they grasped the perilous nature of them. For centuries they had lived with humans and had come to understand far more than just "fetch" and "walkies", so when the humans talked of disaster or famine, the dogs knew these were serious and troubling matters.

Slowly the images and news stories became more apparent. The summers were getting noticeably hotter, rain and thunderstorms lasted for weeks and no sooner had one storm passed than another took its place. Whole areas of housing that had been built on low land were continually flooded out each year. Their occupants both man and dog driven from their homes. Flooded also were huge swathes of farmland, their crops destroyed and so food supplies dwindled.

When the winters came, they were far harsher than ever before, and the colder things got, the harder it became for the humans to heat their homes, and all the while we dogs watched on. As each year passed the conditions became worse. The seasons, spring and autumn, seemed to disappear entirely, and the world we knew was left with only freezing winters and blazing hot summers.

Then their power began to fail. The humans' lights and heat no longer functioned when they flicked their switches, they would work only sometimes. And all the while the storms worsened. With the intermittent power, the winters were proving fatal to the elderly and infirm. Countless numbers died in their homes, their pets unable to escape would die with them. Dogs can go without the comforts that humans seemed so dependent on, but even we cannot live without food. There are many stories from this time of pets begging for help at windows, but those dogs that witnessed this from outside were powerless to free them. The cats fared better for they had cat doors through which they could come and go as they pleased, but most dogs were less fortunate, and our numbers dwindled along with our human masters.

Finally, the power stopped and never came back on. No more heat, no more light, but also no more help ever came. Those magnificent cities, once the scene of bright lights and leisure, descended into darkness and chaos. Not safe even for the stray dogs that had previously lived off the abundant food scraps that humans once so carelessly discarded. Now every morsel was precious and fought over by animal and human alike.

While good humans tried to ration and share what they had,

bad humans sought to take what they had not. Roving gangs of robbers stole food from the defenceless. It was demonstrated in those brutal times that the most savage beast to ever walk this earth could be man himself.

Out in the countryside where people had been less dependent on technology, the human societies fared slightly better. Some settlements banded together to form communities and attempted to become self-sufficient, but in the absence of the traditional seasons it was a constant struggle for them to grow food in ample quantities. And while they toiled in their fields, beyond their hedgerows the once great cities succumbed to decay where the dead laid unburied. Famine and disease gripped the land and was spreading everywhere. Then came the final hammer blow for the last vestige of humanity, a great sickness that would be their end.

We do not know exactly what it was, but we dogs suspect it may have been something in the water. All life needs water, humans were no exception, but there was something wrong with it. We could tell it tasted slightly different but while it had no ill effect on us, nor other animals of the world for that matter, the humans fell sick and died. Perhaps the odd tasting water was a coincidence, and the sickness was caused by something else, we will never know for sure. All we do know is that our ancestors had been at man's side as they flourished, now they stood by their side as they perished.

For all those long centuries mankind and their canine companions had lived together as one. Puppies and human children grew up together as siblings. Long morning walks in the crisp air. Family trips to the seaside, splashing together in the waves. Glorious days of sunshine, lounging and playing in parks and gardens. All fading from memory like the waking from a dream.

And so it came to pass that just as that cold and lonely dog in ancient times had stepped nervously towards the firelight, mesmerized by those bright flickering flames dancing merrily in the dark of night. The warmth and light of humankind was extinguished, and the time had come for the dogs to turn away from the dying embers of humanity and walk back into the darkness of the forest from once they had come.

With her story over, Alice fell silent, her head bowed solemnly, and tears of sorrow fell from her eyes for a lost people she never knew but loved all the same. The other members of the Faithful shared her grief, while Lord Hawthorn and the others, whose past was not so entwined with humans, still understood and felt the sadness from this tale.

Then Sweetbriar raised her paw and spoke, "Can there definitely be no humans left?" she asked.

Delphine answered on behalf of Alice, "The world is vast and extends far beyond the confines of our home. We ourselves have seldom travelled far from here, but the birds do so regularly and tell us of their sightings of many things. In our immediate surroundings the forests and hills continue for many leagues, home to ourselves and many others such as yourselves. To the north beyond the ancient wall are the wildlands where wolves and wildcats battle for dominance while mighty eagles watch on from their mountain eyries. To the east are wide expanses of wetlands teaming with fish and fowl and the dominion of the otters. In the west the forest becomes the home of many snuffling boars, before giving way to grassy hills and rocky mountains, home to clambering goats that cling to the steep slopes without fear of falling. And way to the south, far past the flooded city lies the rolling downs where horses and deer roam free. And beyond all these places lie great seas that only the birds can cross, and those that have, report finding yet more land to explore, but for all their travels no news of humans has ever been reported. That does not prove they are not out there somewhere, but if there is a lost enclave of humankind then word of them has not reached us."

"But what of the door" Sweetbriar replied, "Elderberry found a sealed door deep below the ground. Perhaps they went underground to escape the sickness, and even now they still live in some underworld beyond our reach."

"That would perhaps explain why we cannot figure out the mechanism that seals it, if it is opened only from the inside." Elderberry added.

"Nonsense," Lord Hawthorn scoffed, "If humans have been hiding behind that door of yours for over a hundred years, they would've starved to death long ago."

"Do not be so quick to doubt the skills of humans." Delphine interrupted. "For all their scientific achievements, preserving supplies would, I imagine, be a relatively easy task for them. I should like to see this door of yours, we dogs are unmatched in our sense of smell, and if humans are living behind it, I should be able to smell them, I'm sure."

"You are more than welcome to accompany us back to Greenvale and see it for yourselves. In addition to the door, I'm sure Elderberry would like to show you his collection of artifacts, perhaps your knowledge of humans may help him identify some of them." Lord Hawthorn proposed, which met with enthusiastic agreement from Elderberry.

By this time, it was getting late so Delphine invited them to spend the night with the Faithful, and they could set off for Greenvale in the morning. It was a wonderful evening they enjoyed together, exchanging stories, and finding the two communities had so many values in common. They all became the firmest of friends and enjoyed the time immensely, especially Bramble who had found his calling in life as the official ball thrower for puppies, though even many of the adults could not resist the lure of ball chasing and joined in with the fun. So worn out with throwing did he become that he managed to teach the dogs a trick of holding the ball in their mouth and with a flick of the head throwing it themselves. It wasn't very accurate, but at least he could take a break from time to time. Needless to say, when it came time for bed, he slept like a log.

11: CORPORAL SMITH

Seamus kept low as he moved cautiously through the trees to where Sasha lay half hidden on the edge of the woods. As he moved up level with her, she whispered "Over there on the far side of the bridge, something is moving inside that building". Seamus looked out across the open ground towards the bridge that spanned the river about three hundred metres to their front and surveyed the building. A neglected petrol station, some of its former large window panes now broken open to the elements, presumably the work of scavengers looking to loot its contents. And sure enough, something was moving just within its open doorway, though he couldn't be certain as to what. From this distance it appeared as merely a dark shadow. Whatever the case, this bridge needed to be crossed, and that would take them directly past this building, there would be little chance of doing so unnoticed. As confident as Seamus was his team could deal with any threat that may lurk inside the shadows of that building, he had the civilian Freya to consider. His mission was clear, ensure Freya and the package she carried reached their destination at all cost, needless risks could jeopardize that mission.

"What are your orders sir, shall we attempt it?" Sasha enquired. Seamus paused briefly before responding, "No, we shall wait, perhaps whoever or whatever it is will tire of the place and move on".

For several hours they laid there watching intently for a sign this potential scavenger would leave. The hours passed and still there was no sign this mystery movement would abandon its position in the doorway. Seamus knew they could not wait indefinitely, for although the light would fade and crossing the bridge in darkness would provide them some measure of concealment, it would also reduce their awareness of whatever this threat may pose. Finally, he made his decision, they had wasted too much time already. The objective lay on the far side of that river, and it was too wide to try swimming, but rather than all of them chance a dash for it, he would proceed alone and scout out this place before the others followed on his signal.

Breaking cover from the tree line he cautiously advanced across the open ground that ran parallel with the road, halting occasionally to observe and listen before continuing. Within about a hundred metres from the bridge he stepped onto the road itself and crouched by its side. From this closer vantage point he relaxed slightly, for he could just make out the movement he had been so concerned of appeared to be merely a piece of cloth fastened to the door frame and it fluttered freely in the breeze. With no sight or sound of any scavengers, he pressed on, reaching the start of the bridge he began to cross. With no cover on the open bridge, this was the moment of truth, if there were eyes upon him, he would soon know it, yet nothing happened. The cloth in the doorway continued to flutter lightly but no other movement could be discerned. As he reached the far end of the bridge, he could see clearly the fluttering fabric was of camouflage material, the type used for military uniforms. This was no random curtain, but a soldier's combat jacket hung from the door frame for reasons unknown. Seamus approached carefully, ever mindful of what surprises may await. Once he reached the doorway, he hesitated briefly but with no sounds from within he stepped inside.

Sasha and the others watched patiently from the tree line as Seamus disappeared from view. Although he was only inside for a few minutes the wait seemed like an eternity, until finally he emerged again and called them over. Hurrying from cover and across the open ground to the bridge they soon crossed and gathered on his position outside the building.

"What did you find?" Sasha enquired, having noticed the serious expression on his face.

Seamus hesitated to gather his thoughts before explaining. "Three bodies. Now we know why corporal Smith's detail never returned from their mission, his three men lay dead inside. Judging by the position of the bodies and how all three lay in their sleeping bags it looks like they fell victim to either the same thing that has decimated the garrison, or the cold got to them as they slept. Whatever the cause, their mission ended here. They were tasked with finding fuel for the vehicles, but it appears this is as far as they got before death took them".

"But what of corporal Smith himself?" Sasha asked.

"I can only assume he continued the search alone. Two of the empty fuel cans they carried are not here, so I can only guess that it was he that hung that jacket by the door to mark the location of his fallen comrades. We shall do what he presumably lacked the strength to do alone and bury the bodies of our brother soldiers. Then we must continue on our way, if our paths should converge some way ahead then so be it, but regardless of whatever fate befell him we have our own mission to achieve and last winters need for fuel is long past".

The team set to work digging graves in a grassy area behind the petrol station and once done they dragged the bodies out and interred them, still inside their sleeping bags. In the absence of coffins this was the best the team could provide, and after piling the earth above the graves, they stood awhile in silence to honour the memory of their fellow guardsmen. And with that duty complete they assembled back on the road and hurried on their way.

The road beyond the bridge continued southwards and on its flanks were several isolated stands of trees. As they proceeded along its course the trees became larger and more numerous until the road was sandwiched between thick woodland on either side. As the forest closed in on each side of them the road became all the more claustrophobic, but on they went.

Having spent too much time at the bridge they decided to make up for as much lost time as possible by not stopping even when the light of day began to fail. Besides, they all felt they wanted to put as much distance as possible between themselves and that lonely place of death they had just left.

Into the night they continued, not stopping even when it began to rain. For the benefit of Freya they kept a slow but steady pace, but they never stopped completely until finally, about an hour before dawn the road emerged from the forest, and rolling countryside was before them once more. Not far ahead, silhouetted against the night sky they saw the ground on the right of the road rise to a low ridge, spattered with patches of gorse, an excellent place for concealment, Seamus thought. From there they can observe the terrain around them and rest up in safety.

They veered off the road and headed up the slope, keeping low as they crested the ridge so as not to skyline themselves. Once safely in the cover of the gorse some turned to face the road and went to ground while a couple of others continued a short distance over the reverse slope to cover the flanks and rear. There the group waited patiently in the wet ground for the first light of dawn. Every soldier knows that dawn is a time for high alert, for if something is going to happen, it usually comes with the fresh visibility of the morning light.

Even when the clouds parted and the rain stopped, they still could not quite discern the road below them in the darkness. They remained in their positions for what seemed like an eternity but slowly the darkness of night turned to that grey half-light just before the first glow of light dispels the shadows of night completely. And as they scanned the area around them, they could now discern the lay of the land. The road continued ever onward but now bordered not by trees but fences and hedgerows. The forest had given way to more open former farmland, and here and there could be seen the occasional old farmhouse or barn that dotted the landscape. Seamus could see a distant flock of crows circling over one of the silent buildings and he wondered if that also contained nothing but the dead, perhaps even corporal Smith, but finding out was not his mission. With no visible threat in any direction, and with sentries posted they now rested and got what sleep they could, for they must be on their way again by noon.

12: THE DOOR

In the morning Sweetbriar and her friends rose early and found the ground wet for it had rained in the night, though having spent the night under the shelter of trees they had scarcely noticed it doing so. With the sun rising and the ground drying out, the companions bade farewell to their new friends as they prepared to head back to Greenvale. With Elderberries' permission Bramble let Trixie keep the ball she loved so much. Many of the dogs gathered round to wish them safe travels and bade them to come visit any time. Delphine was to accompany them on the journey back, along with a scrappy little terrier type dog named Chindit. He was considered second to none for his sense of smell and if Delphine could not detect the scent of a human behind that locked door, if they were there, he certainly would.

It was a long journey back and would take a couple of hours so again, Sweetbriar and Elderberry rode on Lord Hawthorn's back, while this time Bramble wanted to ride on Chindit. Being a small dog it was easier for Bramble to climb up onto him and Chindit was only too happy to carry the little squirrel. As they made the long walk back, they chatted merrily to one another, sharing stories of events both past and present. So comfortable in each other's company were they that the time seemed to fly, and they soon found themselves cresting the southern ridge of Greenvale and heading down towards Frosthome nestled in the forest.

Their arrival was met with much excitement, for few of the valley had much knowledge of dogs and the appearance of Delphine and Chindit were of great interest to them.

"Welcome to Frosthome Hall" Lord Hawthorn announced, "We can rest here before we take you to the door if you wish".

Delphine was eager to see this door and politely declined the offer of rest. This met with the approval of Elderberry and Sweetbriar for they too were eager to solve the mystery of what may be behind it. Hawthorn was skeptical that anything would come of it, while little Bramble had forgotten all about the door and was simply enjoying the ride. But since no-one needed to rest Hawthorn led them all into the western woods where the slope of the valley ran ever upwards.

As they pressed on, the trees began to take on a younger appearance than the thick well-established forest that surrounded Frosthome. They could see in the bushes and undergrowth the remains of old stone walls that humans had used to mark the boundaries of fields, clearly this area had not always been so wooded. Then they passed through what may once have been a gateway, though only the rusted posts remained standing, the gate itself had fallen from its hinges long ago and now lay buried under the choking mass of thick weeds that covered everything. Still the ground sloped upwards, and they caught glimpses of old buildings amongst the tangled brown masses of bushes and weeds. So covered were they, that was it not spring but summer, the weeds would've recovered their foliage, and these buildings wouldn't even be visible to them. Dotted about they could also see many holes and mounds of fresh earth. These were the sites of Elderberry's many excavations in his quest to understand the history of the old world, but these sites were not their goal. They pressed on passed these old ruins and continued upwards into the tree covered slopes beyond. And finally, they arrived at the entrance to a large tunnel in the side of a steeply sloped bank below some trees.

"Here we are". Elderberry announced, beaming with pride that somebody other than himself and Sweetbriar were interested in his discovery at last, and together they all descended into the passage beyond.

Once past the dirt and rock-strewn entrance cleared by the badgers the previous autumn the tunnel opened into a perfectly smooth walled passage. Clearly this was fashioned by human hands from materials unfamiliar to the animals of today. It was smooth and polished and had no visible joints in its construction. As they pressed on their eyes became more accustomed to the darkness and they noticed that at regular spacings there were strange devices fixed high on the walls, all identical with a transparent glazing behind which they could see very little for they were too dusty.

"Any idea what those may be, Delphine?" Elderberry enquired.

Delphine examined one as closely as she could, for they were far higher than she could reach. "I'm not entirely sure for I've never seen any myself, but I suspect they were once lights that I've heard humans used to illuminate dark places".

"Humans couldn't see in the dark?" Elderberry responded. This seemed weird to him being a mole, for he always assumed all things could.

"No, they couldn't, we dogs aren't the best at it either, though I guess a lot better than humans were".

They continued down the dark passage until finally, after some considerable distance they arrived at its end where, set in a solid wall blocking further progress, they could see a completely plain and smooth looking door. It had no handle to open it and if it had hinges, they were not visible on this side of it. While the door itself was completely devoid of any sign of mechanism or latch, on the wall next to it was a small rectangular box of a different material that protruded outwards near its base to form a kind of sloping shelf. This was also plain apart from a small, faded symbol of four curved lines of decreasing width, but it showed no mechanism with which to interact with the door. The only thing of note about this was near its top a tiny red light glowed faintly. What human magic powered this tiny prick of light they could not even begin to imagine.

"And here it is, the sealed door" Elderberry announced with a flurry of enthusiasm. "Perhaps now, with your help, we can finally solve this mystery".

Delphine and Chindit stepped forward, each taking an edge of the door and placing their noses against the slight crack they took a long series of sniffs. The others watched on, eagerly anticipating their conclusions. After several attempts the two dogs stepped away from the door. Delphine spoke first to Chindit.

"That's very strange, I could smell nothing at all".

Chindit nodded in agreement, "Same for me, very strange indeed" he replied.

The others were disappointed but also a bit confused. Sweetbriar asked the question for them all.

"I can understand you couldn't smell anything behind that door, but why do you both say it's strange and seem so baffled by that fact?"

"Because the fact neither of us could smell anything is very peculiar indeed. We both have an excellent sense of smell and even an empty room would give off a scent, whether it be damp and musty, or dry and dusty it would smell of something, yet in this case we can smell nothing whatsoever. Whatever mechanism seals this door, it is closed so tightly that not even the slightest odour can pass through it."

"I'm so sorry for wasting your time" Lord Hawthorn apologised, but Delphine assured him he didn't need to. This door was indeed a mystery, and it intrigued them immensely. They were only too willing to help, and the fact it had been sealed so tightly, simply piqued their curiosity all the more. And so, with no answers but more questions, they all turned about and headed back up the passage towards the daylight.

13: THE GOLDEN MAN

The pack had travelled many leagues, and the cold northlands were long behind them. The glens and mountains had given way to more rolling and lush lands the further south they headed. Now they rested, for there was more distance to cover before they would reach their desired hunting ground.

Brasidas sat waiting for the last of the patrols to return. It was the custom when the pack halted to despatch scouting parties to investigate their surroundings. The other teams were already back but Spartan's was long overdue. Brasidas was concerned they may have run into trouble. He had faith in Spartan's leadership, and the skills of his team, but the world could be a dangerous place even for the fiercest of warriors, and who knows what dangers lurk in these woodland realms.

Finally, Brasidas's ears pricked up, something was coming. He sniffed the air and relaxed, but only slightly. Sure enough it was one of the scouts, a seasoned veteran by the name of Fenrir, but concerning that it was only he alone. Fenrir slowed his pace as he approached Brasidas, catching his breath as he came.

"Report" Brasidas demanded, "Where is the rest of the patrol?"

Fenrir cleared his throat before responding. "We found something sir, something odd." He paused briefly before continuing as if trying to find the words to explain what it was, for in truth, he wasn't actually sure himself. "The patrol is waiting back where we found it, a talking stone".

Brasidas was taken aback, he had heard many patrol reports in his time as leader, and he himself had seen many things, but never anything so bizarre as talking stones. "What on earth is that supposed to mean?" He enquired.

Fenrir repeated himself, for he didn't know how else to describe what he had seen and heard.

"Well, what did this talking stone of yours say?" Brasidas asked.

"Keep off the grass, sir".

"And what did you do?
"We got off the grass sir".

Brasidas prided himself on commanding the fiercest warband in the land, and here they were intimidated by a talking stone. He had to see this thing for himself, so leaving Darius in command of the company, and with Fenrir leading the way, off they ran into the woods.

For several miles they went until finally the woods began to thin and they found themselves on what appeared to be an old road. Not large but more of a narrow lane, long cracked by many winters and overgrown by tall weeds that had taken root in these cracks and widened them further. In places the weeds had been so ruthless as to tear away whole sections of the road, and in its place taller shrubs and saplings had thrived. As they continued along this forgotten lane, Brasidas became aware of old buildings on either side, choked by the same weeds that had torn apart the roadway, and difficult to reach without forcing a path through thick sprawling masses of bramble and hawthorn. And there ahead looming above all else the unmistakable tower of an old church. Brasidas had long noted that it seemed the older the human building, the better it had withstood the erosion of nature and age. In his travels he had passed through many ruined cities, yet at their centre he found the most magnificent buildings with ornate arches and decorative columns still standing proud despite the best efforts of the weather, weeds and ivy that clawed at their stones, and ancient castles and cathedrals still towered above the rubble of their surroundings. It baffled him that the humans, whose ancestors were capable of creating such strength and beauty, would instead favour less sturdy constructions towards the end of their long history. The further their buildings extended around the edges of these old city centres, he had found whole estates of human homes now reduced to nothing more than rubble that marked the foundation lines of their former walls. The unchecked elements had made short work of tearing them apart as if they'd been made from straw. But this area in which Brasidas passed was clearly older than those substandard suburbs, it was once a small rural village. Brasidas and his pack had seen countless hundreds of these in their travels throughout the years. A scene repeated every time, a former settlement of human existence, long abandoned and reclaimed by nature.

As they approached the church, he could see Spartan and the rest of the scouting party waiting patiently outside the remains of an arched gateway, the gate itself, presumably once made from wood, long fallen to the ravages of time, but the small roof remained intact atop it's stone archway.

"What's all this nonsense about talking stones, call yourself hunters?" he growled as he arrived. The scouts began to answer at the same time, some spoke of voices, others mentioned magic stones, but they rambled over each other so much so that Brasidas couldn't make head nor tail of what they were blabbering on about.

"Enough" he barked "show me this stone of yours and I'll get to the bottom of this.

Spartan gestured inside the gateway "It's in there sir, you can't miss it, it's at the base of a big cross, a large brown stone just lying there. There are several smaller ones dotted about, but it's the big one that spoke".

Brasidas sighed with exasperation. It's a sad truth that even the fiercest of wolves is afraid of the unknown, they would gladly fight the mightiest of foes, yet hesitate before a ladybird if its spots formed an unfamiliar pattern. Brasidas considered himself above such childish fears, he had proven himself in the field of many battles and would yield to none, let alone a talking stone. And so, he proceeded on alone through the arch.

Nothing could've prepared him for the sight that greeted him. He had seen many ruined churches and overgrown graveyards before, but this was something completely new, or to be more accurate something completely old. There were no weeds and broken walls. Here the grass was cleanly manicured, and the tombstones stood upright and proud. The gravel path that led to the church was pristine, its borders as true as the day it was laid. Even the church itself was largely undamaged. Some tiles had slipped out of place, but without ivy clawing into the fabric of its flint walls it had managed to survive the test of time. Coming through that arch was like stepping back in time, and there ahead, just off to the side of the path was the large cross Spartan had mentioned, and at its base the supposed talking stone.

He slowed his pace as he cautiously proceeded along the path. Once level with the cross he stepped gingerly off the gravel onto the grass for a closer inspection. A good long sniff would tell him if this was stone or not, but before he could get close enough…

"What part of keep off the grass do you not understand?"

Startled, Brasidas leapt back onto the path. A little embarrassed with himself, he quickly looked back towards the gate to reassure himself the scouts hadn't seen his reaction. Unfortunately, they had. A brave leader, startled by a stone, he'd never hear the end of it. He needed to put on a show of strength and courage, so trying his best to swallow his fear of this evil sorcery that confronted him, and in the most commanding voice he could muster.

"I am Brasidas the fearless, and I will not be dictated to by a lump of rock. My jaws shall shatter you to gravel if you don't identify yourself at once" he demanded.

The stones reply astounded him.

"You'll be called Brasidas the toothless if you try it, though I am no rock, I am a tortoise, but my shell is as hard as stone." Then a small head poked out of a hole at one end of the stone like shell and continued "And if you must know, my name is George."

In an instant, a wave of relief washed over Brasidas, there was no magic at work here, just a strange looking yet apparently harmless creature called George. While he had never heard of such a thing as a tortoise, he could tell from its funny little face that it posed no threat. Composing himself and in a warmer tone he continued.

"What is this place, how come it looks so pristine?"

George looked around at the perfectly kept cemetery before replying.

"I like to think of myself as the church warden though

obviously I'm only a tortoise. The real church warden died long ago, but we have been continuing his work ever since. David liked things just so".

As George was speaking Brasidas became aware that the other smaller boulders his scouts had mentioned being dotted about were also tortoises, and they were busy at a snail's pace moving about nibbling the grass as they went.

"David?" Brasidas enquired.

"Yes, David was the vicar here at this church. He brought Geraldine, my late wife and I here when we were young and although Geraldine passed away a few summers back, I have lived here ever since."

This baffled Brasidas. "Surely you mean he brought your ancestors here, not you yourself."

"Oh no" George said, "We tortoises live a very long time. Not sure how long exactly, but needless to say, we see the passing of many lives in the span of our one. Non tortious lives are like fleeting moments to us, they can shine so brightly before fading and being consigned to our ancient memory."

Seeing Brasidas in conversation with this strange creature, Spartan and the other scouts had lost their fear and had slowly approached, though keeping mindful to stay on the path. Now they all sat together alongside their leader. No longer the fearsome fighters they prided themselves as being, but like children gripped by the magic of a storyteller.

And there they sat, mesmerized as George recounted his life in the old world they could never know themselves and had until now only guessed at. He spoke of how the bells would ring and the people from the village would come to be met by David at the door to the church, and when they went inside they would sing. Sometimes they had special occasions when a couple of humans would be the centre of attention with one of them dressed all in white like the most beautiful of swans, and the others would shower them with flower petals. Once a year they would assemble by the cross and lay wreaths of poppy flowers and stand in silence as they honoured the memory of soldiers that fell in wars that happened long before the knowledge of Geraldine and himself. He spoke of how the people would bury their dead in this sacred garden and erected the tombstones that still stand today to mark their final resting place. And then the tales darkened, for over time the funerals became more common, and the number of people that visited the church diminished. With fewer and fewer people to dig the graves, the funerals became less formal, and the ornately carved tombstones were superseded by hastily made wooden crosses. The last funeral to be held was Davids, and afterwards the door of the church was left hooked open for any parishioners that wished to visit and seek comfort in this place of silent beauty. But with no vicar to tend to his flock, the people stopped coming, and yet there George and Geraldine remained to slowly nibble away at the grass and weeds to keep things looking nice. A difficult task at first, but over time they had children that would grow up to share the workload. And they in turn had children of their own who diligently joined the ranks of this ever-growing army of patient gardeners. Beyond the walls of the churchyard a forest of weeds grew up to conceal the outside world from view, but undeterred George and his family continued their work, for being so slow, their world inside this sacred garden was large enough for them. When Geraldine passed, they buried her in the ground where David lay, and when George's turn does finally come he will be placed beside her by his family. This is the way of the churchyard, as it always has been. Maintained by a tireless army of custodians keeping everything neat and tidy, just as David liked it.

Brasidas and his companions had listened intently to every detail of George's story as he brought it up to the present day. So long had they been captivated by his words that all sense of time had slipped from their minds and the light of day was already fading. With the story now told, Brasidas had to ask one more question.

"George, you have seen humans, we have not. Please, could you describe what they looked like?"

George's reply stunned his audience, "I can do better than that, you can see one for yourselves".

Taken aback, Brasidas listened all the more intently as

George continued. "It will be dark soon, the light is failing, but come to the church at dawn and you will see the golden man. He comes every morning, but you must be prompt if you wish to catch him at his best. So for now I shall bid you all good night, and see you in the morning".

It would prove to be a very long restless night for Brasidas and his scouts. They camped outside the gate that night, finding what comfort they could in the mass of scrub around them. He considered sending a couple of them back to inform Darius and the company what was going on but decided not to deny any of them the chance to see this golden man. Despite trying to establish a shift system so that they could all get some sleep, none of them could, they were too excited, for when morning comes they would finally get to see a human. How could any of them sleep and risk missing the opportunity. Brasidas spent the night in wonder, after all these years, those vague shapeless ghosts that had for so long haunted his imagination would finally be given face and form.

As dawn approached, they assembled at the gate and walked back into the dew speckled churchyard. All was quiet and the tortoises were nowhere to be seen. Brasidas led his small group along the path to the church door but halted them outside. He would wait as instructed for the very break of dawn. He did not wish to be late for this appointment but nor did he wish to be rude by appearing too early. And as they stood and watched, the very first glint of sunlight flickered over the distant treetops, and on that cue, into the church they went.

Inside they saw George with his entire family, all facing the same direction, Brasidas and his companions followed their gaze, and that's when they saw him, the golden man. Tall and proud and above all, glorious. His arms open in a welcoming gesture. From around his head golden rays of sunlight fanned outwards and his eyes looked down on each and every one of them with friendship and love. He wore a raiment of many colours which shone brightly in its splendour. This was truly a sight to behold. Finally, those faceless forms of the past were dispelled from Brasidas's mind, never to return, for now he knew the face of man.

But despite the wondrous beauty, this was no living breathing man. It was an image of coloured glass set high in the window arch at the end of the church. The sun shone brightly through each of the multitude of smaller panes that formed this picture of timeless wonder. Splintering into tiny bright shards as it hit the uneven surface of the glass and twinkling like ever moving stars. And then there were the colours. In this weed ravaged world of drab greens and earthen browns, save for the occasional poppy patch and the white flowers of brambles, never before had so many colours been on display at once. Yet here they were, all the colours of the old world framed together in perfect glory. While canine eyes are less capable at perceiving all colours of the spectrum, there were still enough for Brasidas to marvel at. Regardless of the hopes he had as he entered the church, Brasidas was enchanted none the less. This was what George had called the golden man, and it was plain for all to see why.

Then, as if to waken them from a dream, a cloud drifted across the sun and the light of the golden man faded. Brasidas sighed and led his companions out of the church. By the time George got outside the scouts were already gathered by the gate ready to go, they were just waiting for Brasidas who was standing silently by the cross. As George approached him, he turned and spoke.

"This memorial to fallen soldiers, I have heard before of such wars and battles the human armies fought, and how they honoured their dead, we wolves do much the same. They truly must've been a magnificent people, how I would love to someday meet one."

"If you do ever meet one, do not be too quick to trust" George replied "Like all creatures, humans can have many motives, not all of them are good."

"What do you mean?" Brasidas enquired.

George nodded his head toward the back of the cemetery and bade him to look. Brasidas looked and saw a neat row of four smaller crosses set upright near to the back wall. "Those are the graves of four such fallen soldiers whose flying machine crashed in a nearby field" George said, "buried with all the honour and ceremony soldiers deserve, but these were the enemy in one of the many wars this memorial represents. However, if you dig down you will find not the bones of monsters, but those of ordinary men. For all your admiration of the humans, who did you think they fought if not each other. And so, should one day you ever finally get to meet some, remember this…

"Two armies meet for a fight, both are fearless and strong, but if one of them stands for what's right, then the other can only be wrong."

Brasidas thought for a moment, then asked, "But how will I know which one is right?"

"Ah, the age-old question, and for that I can only tell you what David used to say about such things, let your conscience be your guide."

And with that, Brasidas knew he must go, so he bade farewell to George and returned to the others, and away they went, heading back to the main group and the resumption of their great hunt. As they travelled, they continued to talk in awe of what they had seen, and Brasidas decided that although traditionally scouting parties were typically formed on an ad hoc basis, due to the special bond they had formed through witnessing the wonder of the golden man, from that day forth Spartan's team would become the company's permanent reconnaissance unit.

14: THE SHINING STAR

It was now mid-April, and the green shoots of new leaves were emerging from the buds on the trees and soon Greenvale would be fully green again. The weather was wonderful, and the frozen winter and early spring frosts were a thing of the past. Now life was returning, not just to the plants, but the animals themselves were feeling rejuvenated by the warmth of the sunny days they now enjoyed.

It's been three weeks since Delphine and Chindit had visited to see the door and they had stayed a little longer than planned. So intrigued were they by its secrets that they'd spent a few days searching the surrounding area for any sign of a back door or other form of entry. But there was nothing to be found, the only entrance was that single sealed door that seemed impossible to breach. Eventually, she and Chindit had to concede defeat and with regret bade their new friends farewell and returned home.

Since then and with the coming of warmer weather all thought of the door had diminished. Lord Hawthorn's work parties finished off the last of their repair jobs around the valley. Elderberry had gone back to his excavations, while Sweetbriar and Bramble had resumed their work examining the various objects he unearthed.

One such object was a small, almost flat metallic item shaped like an eight-pointed star. She picked it up for closer inspection, turning it in her paws and carefully rubbing the soil from its surface. Beneath the dirt she found no rust like so much else of the artifacts Elderberry had discovered, this was bright and shiny as if new. She couldn't imagine something remaining so pristine after a hundred years in the ground, this was a strange metal indeed. Looking closely, she saw its surface was raised slightly to form images and within the star shape was a circular band upon which strange symbols could be seen. Sweetbriar had no clue what human letters meant but she had seen enough objects with similar markings on to at least recognise them as being human. And at the centre of this circle, she could make out a diagonal cross over which was set what appeared to be some kind of leaf, similar in shape to clover. Turning the object over she found to its concave back was attached only a flat plain bar that bore no markings at all. Perhaps this was once used to fix it to something she thought, though what to and why she could not guess. Having never seen a human, Sweetbriar had no idea they wore clothes, and lesser notion still that sometimes they wore things purely for decorative reasons alone. What she perceived as a strange shiny star, had once been worn by a long dead human with pride. Placing the item back on the ground she turned her attention to the next.

15: PHINEUS

The Scouts felt claustrophobic as they moved cautiously through the forest. There was an eerie silence in this area that made them feel that some danger lurked close. Spartan led as they pressed on, his ears and nose on high alert for the slightest sense of trouble. There was definitely something not right about this place, they all felt it, and it made them uncomfortable. Why was there no sound, where were all the animals and birds, how could a place be so deathly quiet?

Then suddenly, Spartan froze, the scouts that followed did the same. He peered intently at a thicket of twisted brambles for something had moved within. Then a small croaky voice spoke.

"I wouldn't go any further if I were you, or the sirens will get you."

There, sitting on a fallen tree limb nestled in the brambles sat a toad. Spartan approached slowly to address it.

"What do you mean by sirens?"

"Well, to be honest, I don't really know what they are, but if you keep going the way you are, you'll hear them soon enough. And then you'll have a choice, turn back or keep going, and if you choose the latter you'll not return, nobody ever does."

"So you don't actually know the fate of those that went toward the sound since none returned to tell of it." Spartan enquired.

"I do not, but it is a safe assumption that no good came of it. This area was once teaming with life, a safe and happy place under the protection of a great blue boar, but all that changed when the sirens came. Their song echoed through the forest and our champion went to investigate, but alas he did not return. Since that day some brave souls have dared to follow the siren call if only to discover his fate, and like him have also never been seen again. With all the large animals lost to the sirens, the smaller creatures abandoned this cursed place and fled in search of a safer home, and now, I alone remain to warn off unfortunate travelers such as yourselves."

"If these sirens of yours are so dangerous, why would you take such a risk?"

"Oh there is no risk to myself, after all, would you eat a toad?

Spartan thought for a moment. Whatever fate befell those that went further, while concerning, it did need investigating. He and his team were scouts after all, their purpose was to scout the terrain ahead of the company, and gather all intelligence they can. If there is something ahead that could pose a threat, he and his companions needed to find out what.

"I thank you for your warning brave toad, but our duty lays ahead. Fear not however, whatever danger awaits, we wolves are more than capable of dealing with it."

Having reassured the toad, Spartan then proceeded to lead his team on through the trees. As they walked Fenrir spoke to Spartan, "I understand your curiosity, but are you sure we have time for this. If some danger lurks ahead, could we not just avoid it and find a different route?"

"This is not a matter of curiosity, even Brasidas himself would agree with me on this. If some unknown terror lurks in these woods, who's to say it will be content to stay here. What we avoid today, we may find ourselves facing tomorrow, and I for one would rather face danger to my front, than have an unknown peril stalking my back".

On they pressed through the oppressively silent forest, listening intently for any sound of these so called sirens, until finally, as if triggered by their approach they heard it. A song of sorts but not a pretty one, a chorus of birds making a shrill garbling sound. Not of such beauty as to attract admiration, but certainly a lure to the curious. They continued cautiously toward the sound.

Passing through the trees, they found themselves approaching a small clearing dominated by a single large oak tree. Stopping before the edge of the clearing so as to remain concealed they surveyed the area. In the branches of the tree they saw nine magpies, singing their unpleasant song, but at the base of the tree there were a few thickets of gorse bushes but in an open area they saw the remains of several animals. Some of these bones were of large creatures such as boar, dear and fox, too large to be the victims of magpies. Spartan knew this and looked carefully at the surrounding bushes. Magpies will steal eggs from nests, or attack tiny fledglings, but even the largest magpie could not bring down a boar. Clearly some other beast was at work here.

"Stay back" Spartan whispered to his team "I shall proceed alone but be ready for trouble."

Stepping forward into the clearing, Spartan did his best to conceal his apprehension. If he was to lure out this beast, he needed to appear an unwary victim. He walked towards the magpies but stopped short of the area at the base of the tree where the bones lay.

"Who dares interrupt our song, step forward so we may get a better look at you." demanded one of the birds, with an authoritative air.

Spartan remained where he was and replied.

"There are many bones here, is there some danger in this place?"

"Forests can be dangerous places, but these bones are old and the beast responsible is long gone, so set aside your concern, you have nothing to fear from us for we are only humble magpies, now please, come forward".

Knowing they were trying to get him into position for an ambush, Spartan did as requested, but he had not dropped his guard and was ready for the expected strike from the nearby bushes. As soon as he stepped forward, the magpie cried "Now" and on that cue a large hulking beast lunged from the undergrowth, though it did so more clumsily than Spartan expected. Already anticipating this attack, Spartan leapt to one side and turning his head, closed his mighty jaws onto the neck of this thing as it passed him. Biting so deep as to inflict a fatal wound but letting go as it stumbled so as not to be dragged down with it. With the loss of their champion the magpies lost their bravado and took flight in panic, squawking insults as they left.

Spartan looked down at the dying beast and realized with

horror what it was. There before him lay a wolf, breathing heavily as its life slipped slowly from it. And worse of all, this wolf was clearly blind, for empty sockets lay where eyes should be. Then it spoke:

"Who should I thank for freeing me of this torment? Though I am blind, my other senses are finely tuned, and I could tell from your scent that you are fellow wolf."

"My name is Spartan, to whom do I speak and why would you attack one that meant you no harm?"

Suppressing the pain of his wound the blind wolf began.

"I was once known as Phineus, though none have called me that name in a long time. I was born into a great company of wolves, all renowned for both strength and fighting skills, and of all of them, I was the strongest, or so I thought. In truth I had the biggest weakness of all: vanity. Believing my strength the most important attribute of a wolf I was unable to understand why others were promoted above me. The company valued leadership over strength, and although I still had eyes in my head, I was too blind to see it. When my own brother Darius was promoted, something inside me snapped. My anger took hold of me, and I attacked him, but because he loved me, he refused to fight, and in that moment I struck him down, killing my own kin. From such an act there is no return. In grief and guilt, I fled into the night, never to return to my beloved company. For many years I wandered the world, alone and disgraced until finally after many long travels I found myself here in this place. Taking my rest beneath this tree in this peaceful forest, I pondered my guilt and wished only for death, and it was here they found me, those accursed magpies.

Landing in the branches above me they somehow guessed my worst aspect, my vanity, and set about appealing to it. Commending me on my strength and my clear fighting prowess they ensnared my mind. Captivating me with flattery they suggested I could help the innocent creatures of this forest that are being terrorized by a giant blue boar. A mighty fighter such as I should have no problem defeating this monstrous beast, they assured me. I lapped up both the compliments and the challenge.

Their plan seemed so straight forward, they would lure the beast out into the open where I would defeat it. Such an easy arrangement seemed ideal, and so I agreed to their proposal. Little did I know I was walking wide eyed into a trap. Sure enough, after a short while, drawn by the sound of their song, the boar came through the forest. Stepping into the clearing, a huge silvery grey creature that looked almost blue when the sunlight flickered on his coat. I was ready for him, "Your reign of terror ends this day" I declared and charged without giving him time to respond. I still remember the look of confusion on his face by this, but there was no time for further words, such a foe must be attacked with speed, I would give no quarter to this fearsome adversary. The boar reacted with lightning reflexes to avoid my initial attack. He was indeed an impressive fighter himself and his speed caught me off guard. Turning to face me he lunged forward with his brutal tusks. Gouging my flank, I managed to reel back before leaping onto his back and sinking my jaws deep. We fought like this for what seemed like an age until finally I gained the upper paw and he fell from his wounds. But as he died his final words have haunted me ever since.

"Why have you slain me wolf? I sought only peace in this forest, and now will the mild creatures I have for so long protected fall victim to your wanton aggression also?"

I could provide no answer, for my own wounds were also deep, and I collapsed into a state of unconsciousness, and that is when the true malice of those evil magpies was unleashed upon me. They had not wished me to save the forest from a terror, their plan was to rid it of its greatest defender. And not content with their vile plan, they still had a sinister use for me. As I lay unconscious, they swooped down and blinded me with their beaks before returning to the high branches so in my dizzy sightless state I could not retaliate. These foul harpies had destroyed me for their own wicked ends. Now, unable to find my own way in the world, I would be their slave. Forced to kill whatever creatures they lured before me, and unable to find food for myself, reduced to living off the scraps they chose to discard. I should've refused to serve their will and allowed myself to starve, but I was too weak willed to do so. And so, that has been my miserable fate, a form of retribution against one that would slay his own brother and a noble boar to satisfy my own ego, now reduced to slavishly killing any other brave souls that followed. A tragedy worsened by the fact that without eyes I cannot even weep for the innocent lives I have so cruelly taken. You my friend have finally ended the suffering I lacked the strength and courage to finish myself."

Spartan chose his words with care. "I am of the same company as you Phineus, though I am too young to remember you personally for I was only a pub when you left. However, your tale is all the more tragic for what you do not know, your brother still lives. Your attack only injured him and although his wounds were severe at the time, he later made a full recovery. Darius now serves as the company's second in command under Brasidas. Had you not fled you would've known this."

"Darius lives? This news brings so much light to my dark heart, though it grieves me that my later sins have been so needless. For these I deserve no pity, but please, may I ask one final favour of you?"

"Name it Phineus, if what you request is in my power, then it is yours".

"The company had a tradition of burying our dead, I assume that tradition still holds. Would you please honour it when I pass. I would find no peace in Wolfhaven knowing my body was still feeding those foul carrion".

"Of course I shall if it comes to that, but first we should focus on uniting you with your brother. I shall send runners back to fetch him, though it would take some time for him to arrive. I shall remain with you until Darias can get here." But Spartan's proposal went unanswered for Phineus was dead.

Calling forward the rest of the scouts, they set to work digging a grave with their paws and into it they placed Phineus. Covering him with a mound of earth they stood a while in silence according to their ways. Though not the bones of wolves, they also buried the other remains, for whatever these creatures were, they did not deserve the fate they found in this place of misery and death. Then, with no more reason to remain, they turned about and returned the way they had come to rejoin the company.

It was some hours later that they passed through the sentries and Spartan went to deliver his report to Brasidas, requesting that Darius also be present, and waiting for him to arrive before recounting the events that had occurred.

Once finished, Spartan and Brasidas looked at Darius who had listened in silence taking in every word, he paused for a moment before speaking.

"My brother's betrayal injured me deeply, but to learn of his fate injures me deeper still. His attack against me all those years ago confused us greatly, for in all the history of our company, none had put personal ambition above duty until Phineus, and nor has any done so since. Raised as we are from pups to believe in duty, loyalty and honour, we could not comprehend the cause of his actions so assumed some madness had afflicted him. Whatever the cause we all agreed he had no place within our company if so afflicted and would not be welcome back. Nevertheless, he was my brother and I loved him still, so I had always hoped that someday he would return to us recovered and I could forgive him, but now I learn this cannot be."

Brasidas, who until now had not spoken, then made a suggestion. "This place Spartan spoke of is south of here and our course still takes us in that direction, you can at least give Phineus your forgiveness at his graveside if you so wish it."

"I would sir, thank you, and I shall do for him what he could not do himself, I shall weep for the innocent lives he took".

16: THE GUESTS ARRIVE

The valley was full of excitement for Lord Hawthorne had arranged a party to celebrate the better weather now that May was fast approaching, and he had invited the Faithful to join them. The animals were busy gathering supplies for the next day's feast and the guest chambers in Frosthome Hall were being prepared with fresh bedding.

Sweetbriar was in the woods looking for anything edible when Bramble came scampering up to her in great excitement. "They're coming, they're coming" he cried. Sweetbriar immediately forgot her search and ran after Bramble as he bounded back towards Frosthome. When they arrived, they were thrilled to see a great many of the Faithful had come. Delphine and Chindit were there of course, plus many other adults, and most excitingly for Bramble many puppies had come along including Trixie. He immediately darted towards her and with the other puppies following they shot off to play.

Delphine addressed Lord Hawthorn who had just emerged from the hall, "Greetings Lord Hawthorn, it is so good to see you again. My apologies on behalf of Alice, while she would love to have come, unfortunately the distance is too great for one of her age."

"I understand completely, age catches up with us all eventually, I'm no spring chicken myself" He replied with a smile.

A great many introductions were made between the Faithful and the residents of Greenvale, and they sat down for lunch together while sharing stories. Some of the Faithful had heard from Delphine and Chindit of the mystery door and were keen to sniff it for themselves. Elderberry was most pleased to let them try and escorted them to it. Unfortunately, the results were always the same, they could smell nothing whatsoever from beyond that door.

But this only served to pique their curiosity all the more. What secrets lay behind this mysterious door? Who sealed it and why? And the most important question of all, how can it be opened?

As these questions remained unanswered for the time being they could only return to Frosthome disappointed, but undaunted. Assuring themselves the answers will come to them someday.

With the preparations for the party complete, and all the guests comfortably quartered the conversations and friendly banter continued well into the evening, but as dusk turned to darkness, they all began to retire for the night, for they would have a busy day tomorrow. If only they knew just how busy it would prove to be.

17: D DAY MINUS ONE

The team was resting outside an old abandoned barn. They didn't risk entering, for its rotten roof beams were barely holding together and could cave at any moment. Not that it could provide much shelter anyway as most of the tiles had long since slipped and fallen. But most importantly for them, as there was no food here, there was little chance of being discovered by scavengers.

Since setting out, the team had taken great care to avoid contact with anyone or anything at all costs but doing so had slowed their progress greatly. Now however, they were getting close to their objective. Seamus paced the area alone thinking of the morning ahead. This time tomorrow his mission will be complete. Will there be rest ahead, or yet another mission, he asked himself. An army life can be a demanding one, but also rewarding for the satisfaction it brings is well worth the effort.

He looked over at his team and felt a swell of pride, for it was a privilege to have been placed in command of such a fine bunch. Even the civilian Freya had kept pace without complaint. He walked over to join them.

"Tomorrow, we make the final move on our objective" he began, "We have come far, and never wavered from our duty. You all know the importance of what Freya carries and can take great pride in yourselves for this achievement. But remember, we represent one of the army's prestigious royal regiments of guards, so when we arrive, conduct yourselves as such. Don't let the completion of our mission go to your heads, I'll not have a display of revelry like some ill-disciplined rabble."

The others laughed for they knew full well that joking aside, Seamus had full confidence in them. It was to be a long and difficult night, for being so close to the end of such a long trip, none could sleep easy. What would the morrow bring? They settled down as best they could, eyes closed but minds busy with anticipation for the break of dawn.

18: WAITING FOR DAWN

The company had travelled far since that first glimmer of spring had spurred them from their winter quarters. While that chance encounter with a raven last autumn had inspired Brasidas to head south in search of an intriguing sounding valley, the raven gave little detail of the exact location, so they had meandered their way down the country searching this way and that, and still had no idea how far they had yet to go. All they really had to go on from the raven was a vague description of the place and its immediate surroundings, plus the tip that if they reached the flooded city they would've gone much too far.

The company was camped for the night at a derelict rural railway station, finding what comfort they could on the hard stone floor of the former platform. Judging by the ornate cast iron work supporting the platform roof and the functional yet sturdy looking brick station house, Brasidas guessed it was very old, and the fact the windows had been boarded up and the rails removed, it had clearly been closed long before the great catastrophe.

Sentries had been posted further out in each direction along the former route of the old line and others were patrolling further afield. Brasidas and Darias walked the moonlit platform in silence ensuring all was well and taking care not to disturb the sleeping wolves. The platform itself extended way beyond the cover under which so many rested and they continued walking to its end. There they stopped and Brasidas turned to Darius.

"What troubles you, my friend?" Brasidas enquired "I've known you long enough to know when something is bothering you."

Darius paused briefly before responding. "I have served you faithfully for as long as I can remember sir, and in all that time you have never failed us."

"I sense a BUT coming" Brasidas interrupted.

"It's just that, don't you think you're putting too much

hope in this valley we're looking for? The company has travelled far and will follow you wherever you lead, but they don't have as much faith as you that this will be the one. The constant disappointment is gnawing away at morale and I'm not sure how long we can hold the company together sir. I sometimes think, what if we just stopped? For too long we've lived by the mantra, we are hunters therefore we hunt. Half the time it seems we're not even sure what it is we're actually hunting for, just this vague belief that we'll know it when we find it. Do you remember, back when you were a pack leader under Pericles' command, and I your Sergeant, we wasted a whole year searching the east coast for a red and white stripey lighthouse that allegedly served as a landmark to a possible hunting ground. Only to discover we were twenty years too late and both it and much of the surrounding area had fallen into the sea long before we got there. And now what are we doing, searching for a valley simply because a raven told us there is one. And why put faith in the word of a raven anyway? I don't trust them, remember the rhyme we all learnt as pups?"

Where Yoemen guard the great king's gold, and Raven's eyes stare dark and cold.

While submerged streets hide watery graves, the tower looms above the waves.

The wealth of kings lies safe and sound, in a flooded vault below the ground.

But in that place no paw shall tread, for death awaits us there instead.

"Sure I remember it, but that's just an old nursery rhyme created to deter youngsters from venturing too far into flood waters, it doesn't mean ravens will harm us. Besides, have you ever known a wolf to be brought down by a raven".

"No, but magpies blinded my brother, and they are not as large as ravens. But even if it is just a nursery rhyme, I still don't trust them and if this lead turns out to be another disappointment, there'll just be another pointless search for another supposed perfect hunting ground just because that's what we do. It's becoming an increasingly hard sell to the company."

Brasidas remained silent for a moment while he formulated his words.

"I know what you mean for I feel it too. There comes a point in every wolf's life when they would wish only to stop. To settle down somewhere and abandon all notions of endless travel and hunting, but what would we do instead?"

"I don't know sir, anything, farming."

"What do you know of farming, Darius?"

"Alright, maybe not farming, but anything other than this endless wandering."

"I wish it was that simple but sadly it's not our choice to make, while our company remains so too does the hunt, it's what we are and why we exist."

"And what will you do sir, when your retirement comes, will you take your place in the rearguard and continue following the company until age overtakes you and you can follow no more, or settle down somewhere and pursue your true interest, your fascination with human history?"

"You know about that?" Brasidas was surprised.

"We all know about it sir, we can't help notice how keenly your eyes light up when you catch sight of anything human related. It's not something to be ashamed of, we all have our dreams and ambitions of things other than hunting, and for you its human history. Perhaps someday, when we retire, we can concentrate on something for ourselves for a change. I for one actually love swimming and when I can no longer serve the company and even training pups in the rearguard is too much for me, I'd like to settle by a lake or river somewhere and splash away my remaining years in the summer sun."

"I thought I had hidden my obsession with humans so well, but to correct you slightly Darius, it is not their history that fascinates me, but rather the notion that there may yet still be some surviving humans out there somewhere. It is the idea of actually meeting one that grips my ambition so fervently. You see, all my life I've had a recuring dream. In it I am a pup again, though not in the rearguard, but in an actual human home with all the comforts and joy that entails. It is always the same, I am seated on a sofa watching the clock above the mantel, its slow hands ticking away yet my concept of time is meaningless. I'm always waiting, waiting for my human mistress to return home from work, but when she does, she has no face for I cannot picture what she looks like. She is devoid of features, no eyes, no mouth, no nose, not even a single hair on her head. And then she fades before me into nothingness, and I wake. I had hoped that after seeing the golden man my dreams would be different, they were but not how I'd wished. Now when she comes home her face is flat and made of glass. The light shines through but she is cold to the touch. I want to love my mistress but I just cannot find it in myself to do so, and then, as always, she fades from my sight and is gone."

"That sounds awful, a real nightmare sir".

"Oh no, it is awful but it's not a nightmare, I don't wake up afraid, I just feel sad. I only wish I could one day see an actual living breathing human and give a face to the mistress of my dreams. But enough about me, more importantly, what will you do when you get command. Will you continue the hunt wherever it may lead?"

"Of course sir, of that I am certain, the hunt will continue to it's very end. But I must confess I don't think I could ever muster as much enthusiasm for vague leads as you do, my hunting methods may prove more of a slow plod than a forced march. But on that score, there is another issue that troubles me. An issue that probably troubled you also before you took command. If the company should finally find what we are hunting for, what happens next? Should our search prove successful, will there still be a company to command?"

Brasidas smiled, "There is nothing wrong with slow plods, at least they can be methodical and give less chance of missing something important. You will make a fine leader of wolves and bring your own way of doing things as did all the leaders that have gone before. You shall earn yourself great renown I am certain, and as for what next for the company should we succeed, well I'm sure there will always be something worth fighting for".

Brasidas then looked at the night sky, "It is almost time, we should head back" and with that they turned around and headed back along the platform. As they passed the sleeping wolves, they stopped over the she-wolf Kassandra, her paw resting gently on the limp lifeless puppy she carried with such care and attention. She was flanked by a pair of alert wolves appointed as her protection detail. Brasidas and Darius both looked down at her with pity in their eyes.

"How much longer will she carry that wretched thing?" Darius asked softly so as not to wake her.

Brasidas remained silent for he had no answer. How long indeed he thought, only fate could answer that. They walked on, back to the other end of the platform. It was that direction the scouts were due back any moment. Brasidas looked out into the darkness, scanning for any sign of movement.

"I wonder what mischief Spartan has been up to this time. I never know what to expect when he's out on patrol".

"He can be a bit spontaneous at times but he's a good lad is Spartan." Darius replied warmly.

"That's the problem, he has a tendency to be too good, allowing his heart to rule his head. Remember the time he brought back that orphaned otter and insisted we raise it in the rearguard until we find an otter family to adopt it?"

"Indeed I do sir, and a fine little recruit he turned out to be. He was a cheeky little rascal, but was always eager to learn the ways of the company, though perhaps better in the water than on the field of battle." Darius responded with a smile.

"That may be, but we're supposed to be a band of roving hunters, not the travelling orphanage Spartan would have us become if he had his way".

"Come off it sir, don't pretend you didn't approve. Spartan's soft spot for little ones is not unique to him alone. You were as cut up as the rest of us when we finally had to say goodbye to little Ollie and release him into the care of that family of otters we encountered in the wetlands".

"I confess I do miss the boisterous little tyke, though he'll be fully grown now, and has no doubt reverted to his natural mischievous ways. Releasing him back into the care of his own kind was for the best. We have been condemned by birth to this nomadic life of constant wandering, it is both our fate and our curse, and we have no right to impose this life upon those not born to it."

"It was our ancestors that set us on this path sir, so we can only pray to their memory that it shall someday end."

"I always do my friend, I always do" Brasidas replied solemnly.

Some twenty minutes had passed when they finally caught sight of Spartan and his team coming in through the sentry point up ahead. Spartan quietly approached to deliver his report.

"We pushed out eastwards as instructed and while the ground is initially slightly rolling it becomes distinctly flatter the further east we went before opening up into a wide expanse of open plain, we found nothing that matches the raven's description. We did however find something of note, tracks. Some force moves parallel with us on a southerly route along that plain, though slightly further ahead. I could not determine their strength however, for they had long passed before our arrival and appear to be taking great care to conceal their presence."

Brasidas found this concerning, what manner of host was out there he pondered. Though it would not deter him from his course, he'd rather not stumble blindly into battle if one can be avoided. He turned to Darius.

"We shall continue southwards at dawn as planned, but summon the pack leaders to me, they must be briefed on this situation and ensure they are ready for whatever we may encounter out there. The company shall head out at first light, and Spartan, I want you and your team to set off well before us so get what rest you can. And remember, you are to observe and report only, no heroics".

19: THE CALM BEFORE…

The open fields below the forest had been used for the morning's games and competitions but now it was time for the final phase of the morning's festivities before the great feast. The telling of stories. It had been decided that along with their new friends from the Faithful community it would be a great idea to share the stories of their respective histories, both Faithful and Greenvale alike, for the benefit of all. The gathering was large and consisted of many different animals. Not just badgers, dogs, squirrels, and moles but all sorts including rabbits, hedgehogs, hares and mice. Even a few of the local foxes, usually content to keep their own council, were in attendance.

In the centre of the growing congregation was set a circle of logs to form an amphitheatre in which the chosen speaker could address the crowd when their turn came. For the moment, here stood Lord Hawthorn awaiting the assembly to get settled, and as they did so he raised his paws to gain their attention and announced the first speaker. This honour went to Delphine who would stand in for Alice on this occasion and recite the fall of man. It seemed only fitting that the first story to be told should be that of the human world and the great catastrophe which pathed the way to the creation of their own.

Delphine took great care to recite the story exactly as Alice had always told it word for word. The way it had been passed down through the many generations that preceded her. The animals of Greenvale listened intently for this was a tale they had never heard before, and knowledge of the humans and their world had faded from living memory. They shared Delphine's grief as the story drew to its conclusion and sat in silent contemplation for a moment, not sure whether to applaud her for the telling of the story, or to weep for the tragedy of the tale.

With her tale told, Delphine moved aside for the next speaker, and up stepped young Sweetbriar. Lord Hawthorn had personally selected her for the task of telling the story of

Acorn. Having been so impressed with her recounting of the tale previously to the Faithful he wished for her to have the honour once more. But even with that experience behind her, Sweetbriar still felt nervous about doing so again, particularly in front of so many that already knew the tale and would spot an error if she made one.

Nerves aside, she needn't have worried. Her telling of the tale was extremely well appreciated, and the little ones enjoyed it immensely. They had all heard parts of the story to some degree from their parents, but this was the full version that fully explained their origins and put context to the community into which they were born. To a round of hearty applause from the crowd Sweetbriar's tail swished with embarrassment as she sheepishly stepped back to make room for Elderberry who was eager to take his turn.

Elderberry stepped forward beaming with pride for he had spent the last few weeks working on a story of great excitement and adventure that he was sure the children would thoroughly enjoy. Baffled as he was by what mysteries lay behind that sealed door of his, he had decided to simply invent a story purely for the benefit of entertainment, and entertaining it certainly was.

What his story lacked in fact was more than compensated for by the addition of a lost Dwarven realm buried deep below the earth. Beyond that sealed door was an ancient palace carved from bedrock with ornate columns and beautiful fountains. The halls of this palace were filled with countless treasures and in the largest sat the Dwarf king on his mighty throne surrounded by his loyal people waiting for the day they would return to the surface world and live in harmony with the animals above. This fictional subterranean world and its people was captivating to the little ones. Bramble and Trixie listened in wonder as Elderberry narrated stories of dwarf battles against formidable monsters from deeper places where no light ever reaches, but many of the adults were less enthusiastic for his tale. This was supposed to be a chance to educate the young with facts not fantasies, but even they could see the pleasure the little ones were getting from the tales and could not bring themselves to intervene. When Elderberry brought his story to a close the children clamoured for more, but he had to politely decline for there was a limit even to his imagination. As he stepped back Lord Hawthorn returned to the centre where he was due to deliver an account of the works carried out during the spring cleanup, but before he could begin there was the sound of a commotion from the back of the congregation. Confused by the interruption, Hawthorn gently pushed through the crowd to where the disturbance was coming from and as he did so he could tell the animals were alarmed by something they had seen way off down at the eastern end of the valley.

Emerging from the crowd he gazed into the distance and was at first confused by what he saw. There at the low end of the valley yet working its way upwards, was a black wave as if a great tide of darkness was crashing over the old stone walls and bubbling its way towards them. Closer to him he saw a fox frantically running up, panting desperately as it came.

"An army approaches, an army approaches!" it cried out "We are being attacked".

Hawthorn strained his eyes against the distance and sure enough this was no black wave of water, but a seething mass of dark shapes, a countless number of beasts charging up the hill and the distance closing with every moment wasted. He needed to think fast, or they would all be done for. Calling his badgers around him he made a snap decision.

"We shall form a defensive line here, while those unfit to fight will escort the little ones back to Frosthome and try to barricade themselves safely inside".

The badgers quickly fanned out across the field, but even joined by the few available foxes present, there were not enough of them to cover the entire span of the valley floor. Delphine ran over with her fellow dogs.

"We shall join you" she said as she arrived by Hawthorn's side. "Together we may have the numbers to hold them off long enough for the others to escape to Frosthome. I shall send Chindit with them to ensure they make it back safely. He's too small for war but a hardy little scrapper in his own way".

And so, as the badgers, dogs and foxes prepared to hold the hasty line they had formed. Chindit rallied the other animals to lead them back up the hill towards the woods and the possible safety of Frosthome. There was much fear amongst them for no war had ever fallen on Greenvale to their knowledge, and the horrible prospect of it was entirely new to them. Sweetbriar knew to conceal her fear for the sake of Bramble and the other children. Maintaining an air of calm, she reassured them all will be well and ushered them to follow Chindit. With Bramble clambering onto Trixie's back and Sweetbriar by their side off they scurried as fast as their little legs would take them.

Hawthorn and Delphine stood silently next to each other gazing down at the approaching menace, still too distant to identify.

"What manner of beasts are these" Hawthorn thought to himself.

Then Delphine spoke as if in answer to his mind.

"Whatever they are, we'll hold them back together. If it's a fight they want, then a fight they shall get".

20: THE DARK TIDE

As Spartan released his mighty jaws, and the blind Phineus stumbled to the ground, the magpies looked on with dismay. With their champion defeated there would be no more easy meals for them. Knowing their game was up, there was no reason to remain, so hurling insults as they did so, they rose as one into the air and flew eastwards in search of fresh pickings. There were plenty of sea birds on the eastern coast and their nests should no doubt provide an abundance of delicious egg-filled pantries for these hungry harpies. But the coast was many miles distant and the journey too great for a single day's flight, so setting their sights on the eastern horizon off they flew leaving the dying Phineus to his fate.

Passing over forests and fields, the land rolled ever onwards into the east and on they flew until after many hours the light of day began to fade, and the dark of night loomed ahead of them. Unwilling to continue their journey by night they landed in the top of a great tree, and here they settled themselves to rest till the sun once more would rise and guide them to their destination. As they nestled together in the high branches, little did they know that unseen eyes were watching them from the ground below, for while magpies are not known for their ability to see in the dark, there are other creatures in the world whose vision is less restricted. Eyes as keen in the dark as if in the broad light of day. Eyes that narrowed to evil slits when focused on their prey.

Oblivious, the magpies settled down to sleep and dream of the plentiful supply of eggs on which they shall soon be feasting, until finally the sun crested the distant horizon, and the first rays of light danced across the treetops. The warmth of the sun stirred them from their slumber and opening their eyes the magpies blinked to gather their bearings. They had landed here in the fading light and had little knowledge of what lay below this tree but there they saw in a clearing at its base lay the fresh carcasses of three dead rabbits. A breakfast platter fit for any hungry carrion and excitedly, down they swooped to peck at these tasty treats. So eager to feed they lost all sense of caution, and not once did they consider who or what had left these rabbits here. Fighting amongst themselves over the food they did not see the danger until it was upon them.

A party of cats had seen them land in the tree that night, but unable to reach them, set about baiting a trap of their own. An ironic outcome for these nasty birds that had so willingly lured other animals to their doom now lured also by their own greed to suffer the same fate. The cats pounced upon them in a flash, and all were brought to the ground in agony as jaws and claws dug into their black and white plumage. The fate of the magpies was sealed the moment they landed in that tree last night, but not all would be slain immediately. The leader struggled desperately against the claws that pinned her to the ground to no avail, and yet no killing blow came. This cat, though preventing her from escaping, made no effort to kill her, but not for reasons of sympathy, compassion, or kindness. No, the biggest and best morsels of any successful hunt must be saved for the leader. The final kill is the privilege of rank. As her companions screamed and died around her, she would have to wait a little longer for her fate to be decided, and that wait would not be a long one for the leader now approached.

The cat that pinned her down brought his face close to hers "Struggle all you can" he hissed "The boss likes to toy with his food".

More cats were arriving and at their head was their leader, Cleon. He stalked over to where the magpie was held and glared down at her. What a feast she shall be, he thought to himself as she struggled against the claws that pinned her to the ground.

"Satisfy yourself with the knowledge that you shall have the honour of feeding Cleon the mighty". He said with sinister glee.

"Wait, I beg you" she cried, desperate for an alternative to the slow yet painful death she knew was coming. "Instead of killing me, let me guide you to something better. There are larger morsels than I in this world and I know where to find them".

Perhaps there was no bartering with this giant wildcat, but even a slim chance was better than none. She was playing for time in the hope that an opportunity to escape would present itself.

"And why should I pay heed to the desperate words of a doomed bird?" Cleon replied, "What could you possibly offer that I could not find and take for myself anyway?"

The magpie had to think fast if she was to talk her way out of this. She cast her mind back to all the many places she had seen in her years of flight and then as she saw the ever-growing number of cats that were still filling into the clearing, she remembered perhaps the ideal place.

"Your numbers are vast" she said "Too vast to be satisfied with the flesh of a few magpies. Armies march on their stomachs and it would take a great number of dead to sustain you. There is a place I have seen, far to the south, where many animals live together in peace. No place of interest to carrion like me for peace leaves slim pickings for those that feed off the dead, but that could easily change if you and your army unleashed war upon them. What defence could peaceful creatures be able to put up against such a formidable force? Release me and I can guide you to this place and once you have finished your fight, there shall be food enough for all."

Cleon listened to her words and pondered the prospect of this place she spoke of. If real, then news of it could not have come at a better time. Since leaving the north he had led his forces down the country pressing every cat he had encountered into his ever-growing army. Fueled by the promise of many kills, the cats had been keen to join him, but as yet they had achieved little by way of victories. He needed to deliver on his promise or risk his army breaking before they even get blooded in battle. If this offer of a peaceful community of animals is true, then an easy victory would galvanise his troops for more. His destination was the flooded city, formerly the human capital where it was rumoured many feral cats still roamed. He knew of this place the humans once called London for there had been a zoo there also. Perhaps some distant relatives of the first Cleon also escaped, and the cats grew large and strong as a result. A powerful and triumphant army marching into London would be a draw to all the rest that seek to bathe in his glory. Then he would be ready to return north and crush those accursed wolves and secure his dream of empire.

Cleon snarled menacingly "You have bought yourself some time bird, if this place of which you speak is real, then take us there and you shall earn your freedom."

"Then let me take flight and I shall show you the way". The magpie replied desperate to be free from the claws that pinned her to the ground.

"Do not take me for a fool, you shall be carried in the jaws of this wildcat here and tell us the way. Your freedom shall come only after you deliver us to this alleged place of peace."

Then one of the wildcats snatched her up in his jaws and with Cleon leading the way the cats filed off through the trees to join the army that awaited them. Had it been lighter when the magpies arrived the previous evening and had they flown just a little further, they would've seen the threat below them. Over two thousand cats of all sizes waiting for the command to move. And now with the magpie acting as Cleon's guide, they gathered themselves up and marched southwards.

It was to take a few days march before the woods through which they passed gave way to more open country. A great expanse of flatness bordered on its western edge by distant rising hills carpeted in green forests. They proceeded through the night for cats cared not for darkness and just as a new dawn was breaking the magpie guided them slightly southwest thus bringing the army closer to the lower foothills of these western peaks until finally, she ushered them to halt just short of the wide entrance of a sloping valley ahead.

"This is the place" she said nodding her beak forwards, "The valley ahead runs westward into these hills, rising upwards as it goes. Narrowing at the far end on the higher slopes it becomes heavily wooded and there you shall find your prey".

Accompanied by a small group of his chosen ones Cleon went forward to see for himself. Keeping low and following the course of an old stone wall he edged closer to the valley mouth. As he pressed on, he could see the land rising upwards to the west and crowned in the distance by thick forest just as the magpie had said, and then suddenly he froze. His eyes focused with callous desire, for there high in the distance in a flatter area before the forest he saw many animals of multiple sizes seemingly playing in the morning sunshine. This really was a prize worth taking, he thought with glee and after observing all he could of the land he snuck back to his awaiting army to brief his troops.

His priority was to prevent any of the animals escaping into the woods to the rear, so summoning the scarred one he had reprimanded so many months before he gave him his orders.

"I said that you shall prove your worth to me or die trying, well now is your chance to do so. You shall take two hundred feral cats and accompanied by a few of my chosen ones, you shall sneak up the northern spur of this valley being sure to stay within the tree line so as not to be spotted and work your way to the rear. You are to position yourselves in the woods at the high end of this valley and prevent any that try to flee, they must remain in the open. In the meantime, I shall move the rest of the army into concealed positions at this lower end and shall begin the attack only once you are in position.

"And how will you know when we are?" The scarred one asked fearfully.

"Because your team shall include this magpie. Once inside those woods, release her and the sight of her in flight will be my signal for the attack to begin".

So as Cleon moved his army slowly forward into concealment, the scarred one and his party began to move carefully up the northern spur of the valley side. It took a few hours for them to reach a point level with the forest before they turned southwards and headed across into the trees that spanned the top end of the valley. Arriving at a suitable spot to secure the tree line, they could not see the animals on the lower slope for they were concealed behind a small ridge that rolled across the slope of the valley, but they could tell they were all below them for there was no noise in this silent forest. All that lived here was in attendance below and none remained in the forest itself. Now was the time to release the magpie but as they did so she fell to the ground in pain.

"Now is your chance for freedom" One of the cats snarled, but having been gripped so tightly had her injured wings and now they gave her nothing but pain.

The cat snarled again "Fly or die, you decide".

She outstretched her wings and with a groan of agony as she struggled against the overwhelming pain lifted herself into the air. Her freedom was short lived however, for as she gained height, her broken wings gave out, and she crashed lifelessly to the ground. And so perished the last of Phineus's tormentors. Although her final effort had not earned her the happy escape she hoped for, it was high enough above the trees to be seen by Cleon and his awaiting army. Their keen cat eyes able to pick out the small black and white flash of the magpie's short yet futile flight. Now the attack could begin.

Cleon had grown impatient waiting for the signal. He had watched as the animals' playing games had ceased their races and congregated together into one great mass. If the signal doesn't come soon, he thought, they may leave and move back into the woods, and he would miss his chance for an easy victory. As long as these animals remained in the open, he could be sure to sweep the field easily. Then at last he saw it. That brief flash of black and white, fleeting as it was, still enough to be unmistaken. "Charge" he roared, and rising from concealment, off they went, hurtling up the slope toward that unaware gathering of easy prey.

With Cleon cajoling from the rear and his chosen ones threatening the ferals forward they went ever upwards. A great wave of murderous intent with eyes fixated on the prospect of all the kills that lay ahead. They would be feasting in this field before the day is out, and nothing would prevent them from doing so, for this was the largest army of cats ever mustered and victory was assured.

21: THE COURAGE OF SWEETBRIAR

With Chindit leading, the party of little animals scurried up the slope towards the forest, Frosthome and safety. As they crested a small ridge that obscured their view of the tree line above, Sweetbriar paused to make sure all the little ones were with them. With the last of them scampering past she looked back down towards the hasty defence line formed by Lord Hawthorn, stretching thinly across the field below. Beyond them she could see the distant great mass approaching. The sheer size and sight of them was terrifying. Tearfully she turned towards the forest and as she crested the ridge the field of battle behind her disappeared from view. On they went, ever upwards and the forest loomed ahead but just as they were almost within it, Chindit abruptly halted them. There just within the forest edge awaited a line of hissing cats blocking their route to Frosthome.

"Fall back to the ridge" he yelled "I shall hold them here".

Running up from the rear Sweetbriar quickly assessed the situation.

"I do not doubt your courage Chindit, but your sacrifice would achieve nothing. You shall be greatly outnumbered and once you fall, we shall be caught in the open to be picked off one by one. No, our only chance is if we make a stand together".

As if from nowhere, something suddenly changed in Sweetbriar. The shy teenage Squirrel found a strength of purpose she never knew existed in herself.

"The enemy has the numbers and as long as they can bring them to bare against us we are done for. Therefore, we must use those numbers against them, funnel them into a place of our choosing where we can outnumber them instead. Hedgehogs! You are too few to form a circle, but a horseshoe shall suffice. Hold as many of the smallest creatures as you can fit while still rolling into balls, your spikes shall keep both you and them safe. No cat would willingly jump over a wall of hedgehogs for fear of getting spiked. The rest of us will make a stand within the horseshoe formation and the gap shall channel the cats in only a few at a time where it shall be us that has the upper paw. We only have to break their numbers to break their will to fight".

Without hesitation the animals did as requested. Mice and moles nestled into the soft fur of the hedgehog's bellies as they curled up into spikey balls in a loose arcing formation. Just within its entrance Chindit took post with Sweetbriar at his side. Next to them stood Trixie for although still a puppy she stood much taller than the others and looked a formidable opponent to any cat. They were flanked on either side by a couple of hares eager to box the ears of any unfortunate cat that dared venture into paws reach. The remaining animals of fighting size spread out to cover the inside perimeter as best they could, while the remaining smallest, Bramble included, took shelter in the centre.

With their hasty defence established all they could do now was wait for the cats to make their move, but strangely, no movement happened. The two opposing groups faced off against one another in an eerie silence.

The cats had watched them form their defensive position yet had not budged an inch from the tree line. Cleon's orders were simple, they needed only to prevent any from escaping into the forest, and the cats' very presence had already achieved this. There was no reason for them to move and so they remained where they were, content simply to observe and await the victorious Cleon's arrival from the lower field.

Truth be told, there were few amongst them that shared Cleon's dream of empire. There would be little if any reward in it for them, for Cleon had no intention of sharing his beloved throne, and they knew it. They also were only too aware that his ambition would never end, he will always desire to expand his empire and that means yet more fighting and dying just to sate his appetite for power. And so, an opportunity to sit on this tree line and do nothing was a welcome respite from the carnage of battle they knew Cleon was unleashing in the lower field.

This waiting game could've easily continued indefinitely

had it not been for the ambition of the scarred one. He needed to prove himself in battle and there was no glory to be had simply sitting on the sidelines watching this group of feeble looking animals taunt them with their presence. The audacity of these creatures that think their pathetic ring of hedgehogs will protect them from his might. Finally, his patience gave way to his ruthless desire and against the better judgement of the other chosen ones he ordered the ferals to attack.

Slowly they stalked forward as all cats do when they corner their prey, but as they closed the distance, they began to rush for the gap that presented itself. The first cat to enter narrowly avoided Chindits jaws but as it did so one of the hares swung a mighty punch that caught it on the chin and sent it reeling backwards onto a nearby hedgehog. Leaping three feet into the air and performing an accidental back flip over the ring of spikes, the cat turned tail and bolted back from the fray. This first victory, though small, was met with a mighty hurrah from the defenders, but there was no time to relish it for still they came.

By pairs the cats tried desperately to force their way into the defensive ring but each pair were either bitten sharply or beaten with many paws before falling back onto those that followed behind. The gap rapidly descended into a confused mass of bruised and beaten cats scrambling over each other to escape the punishment they were receiving. Slowly the initial attack began to wane. The pointlessness of attempting to force an entry this way was dawning on the cats and their reluctance to persevere was showing. The scared one and his fellow chosen ones stalked feverishly amongst the reluctant ferals admonishing their cowardice and urging them forward with threats, but few could muster the courage to enter that accursed gap.

The scarred one was livid. The scars that pock marked his neck from where Cleon's claws had dug so deep, and clearly visible for no fur grew there to conceal them, were red with rage. His first attack was clearly defeated but he still had the advantage of numbers. One of the other wildcats tried to reason with him.

"This is getting us nowhere; we must retire to the tree line and resume our task from Cleon, this pointless assault has achieved nothing". He argued.

The scarred one snapped back at him. "Battle is already joined, do you seriously believe you can slink back to the safety of the trees and still earn Cleon's favour. There is no place for failures by his side?

The wildcats were dismayed by these words for they knew them to be true. Had they done more to prevent this attack in the first place they would've still been in line with their orders, but their failure to do so meant it was too late to turn back. Their only chance now lay in winning this fight before Cleon arrives and then claiming these animals were killed attempting to force their way into the forest. While they would never dare admit it, some even secretly hoped the only thing to come up from the lower field was news of Cleon's death. If he was to fall in battle they could happily pack up and go home, but this was merely a fool's hope and so, setting aside their prior concerns, they resolved themselves to finish this the only way they could, by attacking harder.

22: CLEON'S CHARGE

In the lower valley the situation for Cleon's opening gambit was proving just as difficult. For all his dreams of empire, Cleon was no tactician, he had completely misjudged both the terrain and the capabilities of his troops.

Had he not insisted on marching them through the night they may have had more strength, but even then, that would not be enough for what he demanded of them now. An uphill charge for over a mile with walls and ditches to cross was beyond the stamina of even the strongest of cats. A shrewd leader could've just as easily walked his army up the valley and charged only when the distance was minimal. But no, he lacked the patience for that and now his frantic charge was already beginning to lose momentum, and they were barely halfway there. But on they went, slowing slightly but always forward towards that silent line ahead.

When finally, the front rank of cats crashed into Hawthorn's defence line they were so exhausted their impact was like throwing feathers against a wall. The badgers swept cats aside like skittles with their giant paws, while dogs and foxes grabbed others in their jaws and shook the life from them as if nothing more than rag dolls.

With their impetus lost, the cats threw themselves heedlessly against the unmoving wall of defenders. At the centre of this unflinching line Hawthorn and Delphine fought shoulder to shoulder beating back every successive wave with ease, but still they came.

Cleon cared nothing for the forces he would throw at this line, he would drive it from the field only through brute force so roaring at his exhausted minions, on they fought.

His chosen ones began to take control of the situation at the front. Forcing the feral cats into a rotation system. As each one fell back to recover another would take its place. This allowed for fresh claws to be brought to bear on the line while denying the defenders a respite from the fighting. Badgers and dogs are strong but even they will tire eventually.

23: BREAKING THROUGH

A second attempt at forcing the gap in the ring of hedgehogs had fared no better than the first. Yet another tangled mass of cats beaten back in disorder with nothing to show for their efforts. If the scarred one was to beat this defence, he needed to try something different. Rallying his forces he spread them around the entire perimeter. While none relished the idea of jumping the spikes, his threats of what would happen to them if they did not was enough to drive them to it. They would attack on all sides at once thus forcing the defenders to spread themselves thinner.

Sweetbriar watched the cats fan out to surround them and realised exactly what this meant. In response she left Chindit to hold the gap while tasking Trixie and the hares to act as a rapid response team to deal with any breakthroughs wherever they occur. She and her fellow squirrels would add weight to the fight where they can. Taking up positions within the perimeter just as the cats began to move.

Driven forward by threats from the wildcats the ferals began to slowly stalk forward hissing as they came. Any moment now they would break into a run and come charging forward, but in that moment of tension Trixie suddenly turned to Sweetbriar and spoke excitedly.

"Ball, throw ball" she said.

"Now is no time for games Trixie" Sweetbriar responded abruptly.

"Not ball, rock ball, cats not like it, throw rock ball".

In a flash Sweetbriar understood and stooping to pick up a nearby stone she hurled it with all her might at the nearest cat. Her aim was true, and the stone hit the cat square on the head, knocking it out cold. The remaining cats paused their advance and looked at one another in confusion but as they did so they too were showered in a volley of stones, for following Sweetbriars example all the squirrels began hurling stones as hard and fast as their little paws would allow.

Initially stunned by this barrage the cats withdrew slightly, unsure of what next to do. The scarred one watched on and observed the limited range of the squirrels throwing power. He continued forcing the cats forwards into the hail of stones, only to be beaten back out of range with every attempt, but he knew to keep it up for there had to be a limit to the amount of available ammunition within the confines of that defensive circle.

And sure enough, he was correct, as the squirrels darted this way and that frantically scouring the ground for stones to throw it was becoming increasingly harder to find any. Most of their ammunition had been spent and now lay beyond their reach outside the perimeter. As their firepower diminished the cats were emboldened yet again. Surging forward under the last desperate volleys they began leaping over the hedgehogs and into the waiting defenders.

Fighting tooth and claw the fight descended into chaos. As some of the cats were beaten back, they fell against the hedgehogs and as they did so some were rolled aside. Those that held on to little ones continued to do so, but some of the smaller hedgehogs that were too small to accommodate any mice or moles had felt alone and isolated for too long. Unable to see what had been going on they could only hear the fighting around them, and now as they felt themselves being rolled over they lost their nerve and broke ranks.

With the perimeter now breached in many places and individual fighting breaking out in different places the situation was bleak for Sweetbriar and her companions. Chindit fought ferociously against two of the larger wildcats while ferals clawed at his flanks, but still he would not yield.

Sweetbriar, Bramble and the hares closed together and swiped at any cat that came near. Trixie accompanied by a group of squirrels was giving their all against a surging mass of cats, but they were slowly being driven back under the weight of numbers.

The rabbits fared the worst for having no ability to fight they could only run in panic, but many didn't get far before being bought down under the vicious claws of their pursuers.

Then into the mix he came, the scarred one. Making a

beeline straight for Sweetbriar. Swiping Bramble and the hares aside with his powerful claws and sending Sweetbriar tumbling backwards as he did so. He wished for only one thing, vengeance on this pesky squirrel that had delayed his victory for so long.

"You did this" he snarled as he approached her. "Did you truly believe your tricks could defeat me? All you have achieved is delay the inevitable, now you shall die and I will earn my place by Cleon's side".

Rising to her feet, Sweetbriar frantically looked about her for any stones to throw, If this was to be her end, she would not go down without a fight.

24: THE LINE FALTERS

Cleon's assault had raged for over an hour but finally the results were beginning to show. By rotating the front line fighters, they were better able to manage their strength than the defenders. Cracks were beginning to open up in the line as exhausted badgers, dogs and foxes were forced back under the relentless attack.

Into these gaps the wildcats drove ever increasing numbers to exploit the opportunity to surround those still desperately holding the line. As the situation deteriorated the already fractured line began to waiver. Not yet a broken defence but close to being so, Hawthorn managed to maintain the cohesion of his limited remaining forces and they began to retire slowly. If they can keep the line intact while moving back up the slope where the field is narrower, then perhaps they can establish a stronger position, but to do so would entail edging uphill backwards while fighting off attacks. An army is most vulnerable in retreat and Hawthorne knew it.

The move was slow, ponderously so. Fighting like lions they edged inch by inch backwards. If any should lose their nerve and turn their backs for sake of speed they would be done for. There was no option but to keep their front firmly fixed on the enemy. With the cats throwing themselves onto them in successive waves they edged ever backwards but as they went, with each of their number brought down yet another gap appeared and as there were no reserves to fill them, all they could do was shorten the line by closing in.

Then it happened, a shout rang out from Hawthorns left. "We are being flanked, there on the northern ridge another enemy force has arrived".

Hawthorn and Delphine looked up and their hearts sank. There on the ridge was a giant beast of a creature, an enormous black wolf. And from the tree line behind it came a grey mass of many more, stalking forward into the sunlight, their eyes fixated on the battle before them.

Panic began to take hold in the line at this new

development, but it appeared the cats were oblivious to these new arrivals and their numbers still surged forward and the fighting didn't stop,

Hawthorn and Delphine both knew their meagre forces would have no hope against attacks from two directions but resolved themselves to go down fighting regardless. Little did they realise that their line of fighters stood at the crossroads of history, their gallant stand however, was only a small part of a far larger story than they could ever have imagined. A story that had plodded along for over a hundred years weaving itself into the very fabric of time and was finally drawing to its inevitable conclusion in this very valley they had fought so desperately to defend. But this was not a story of war or battles but of hope and its ending would lift a veil from past events of which they knew nothing and would change their world forever.

25: SPARTAN'S CHOICE

Spartan's scouts had set out just before first light and held a direct southerly course. Moving through the forest, the ground was increasingly undulating as it rolled over many high ridges and low ravines, all shrouded in a thick canopy of trees that reduced visibility to no more than a few dozen yards even with the arrival of dawn.

They pressed on for many miles until just before noon a strange sound could be heard from some distance to their front. Spartan halted the patrol to listen to whatever it was ahead. It sounded like a battle was being waged on the far side of a ridgeline they were ascending, and not wishing to stumble blindly into it they cautiously proceeded at a slower pace.

Atop the ridge, the trees thinned slightly before ending abruptly on the lower slope just beyond the crest. Taking care to remain concealed within the tree line Spartan observed the scene before him. Down in the valley below, he could see a large army of cats battling away at an unflinching wall of badgers, dogs and foxes. At this stage of the fighting the defence line had not yet begun to fracture and Hawthorn's forces were still holding strong.

"So much for a place where animals live together in peace" Spartan thought to himself. Scanning the scene, he estimated close to a thousand cats pressing against the smaller defending force stretched thinly across the valley. Then looking further down toward the eastern end of the valley he also saw a smaller but no less formidable concentration of cats that seemed to be assembling there. To the west the valley continued to slope upwards before the ground disappeared beyond a slight ridge over which he could see the treetops of a great forest that continued upwards beyond it. The geography of this place was a perfect match for the raven's description, so without hesitation he turned to the fastest of his team, a female by the name of Boudica and instructed her to race back to Brasidas with the utmost haste and inform him of developments.

As she sprinted back the way they had come, Spartan

continued to observe the battle that was unfolding below him. Then, as he did so, Fenrir sidled up next to him.

"There are tracks back there leading up along this ridge, a force moved passed here this very morning" he reported, "looks as if they headed somewhere up towards that forest beyond the rise".

Under strict orders not to engage but only to observe and report, Spartan needed to ascertain where this other party were headed and what they were up to. So leaving two further scouts, Ajax and Uther in situ, to await the arrival of Brasidas and the company, Spartan bade Fenrir to lead the way. And with he and the remaining three of his small team close behind, they followed the tracks westwards while remaining well within the trees for concealment.

Moving carefully, they slowly worked their way up along the ridge, listening intently for any sounds ahead. With no desire to stumble blindly into danger, they moved like shadows through the cover of the trees. But as the ground rose, they caught their first glimpse of what lay ahead. Higher up on the slope just before the forest was what appeared to be a circle of defenders fighting off repeated waves of attacking cats, but as they continued upwards, the scene became even clearer, and it was an unusual sight indeed. From within a defensive perimeter of rolled up hedgehogs they saw an assortment of animals fighting as best they could, but most astonishingly, numerous little squirrels launching volley after volley of stones at their attackers. Never had Spartan seen such a thing. Animals using weapons other than their own jaws and claws was unheard of, but most impressively of all, it was working. The cat's attacks were faltering under the relentless pelting they were receiving.

Impressed by what he was witnessing, Spartan continued to lead his group up along the tree line to close the distance and get a better view, but as he was doing so, he saw that the squirrel's volleys were weakening. As their ammunition was becoming depleted the cats were emboldened and began to close in on those gallant little defenders. Still some three hundred meters distant Spartan was enraged as he saw the cats close in for the kill. With the ring of hedgehogs clearly breached the situation was critical. Quickly turning to the others, "Orders be damned" Spartan growled "I've seen all I need to know where my duty lies".

And with no further word, he turned and bolted from the cover of the trees and charged full speed across the open sunlit ground. Without hesitation the other four followed. The time for scouting was over.

26: SACRIFICE

Her eyes quickly darted left and right at the ground about her but to no avail. With no stones to throw, Sweetbriar hardened her resolve. Undaunted she stood her ground against the formidable wildcat, thrusting her forepaws outwards, her tiny claws glistened in the sunshine. And in a bold and determined voice she challenged the scarred one.

"You'll get no easy meal from me, foul beast" and in that moment, with the force of her back legs, launched herself straight up at him. This attack came with such speed and unexpected ferocity that the wildcat was taken completely off guard. Momentarily stunned, he failed to dodge her attack and her little claws scratched deep into his already scarred neck. Reeling backwards from the pain he lashed out and sent Sweetbriar tumbling to the ground. With his neck throbbing the wildcat was incensed by her tenacity. Turning to face where she fell, he hissed "Is that the best you've got fluffball, now feel the depth my claws can dig". And with his rage focused solely on Sweetbriar he pounced.

Dazed from her fall, Sweetbriar looked up as the wildcat leapt, but then as if day had suddenly yet briefly turned to night, a great shadow passed over her. The wildcat was swept away mid leap by the sudden impact of Spartan, but the cat's claws that were meant for Sweetbriar dug deep into Spartan's chest. Initially confused, Sweetbriar saw the wildcat and a wolf tumble away down the slope. Looking about, she saw four other wolves tearing into the remaining wildcats, while many of the smaller ferals were bolting in panic. A wildcat that had been attacking the injured Chindit found itself snatched by the neck in the mighty jaws of Fenrir. Who then proceeded to shake it to death before tossing its lifeless body across at another hapless cat, bowling it over in the process. Regaining her feet, Sweetbriar turned her eyes back down the slope to where her saviour had rolled. She saw that he and the scarred one had slammed to a halt against the rocky remnant of an old stone wall. The wolf lay temporarily stunned but the wildcat was regaining its feet and was now moving against it.

Running as fast as her little legs could muster, Sweetbriar scampered down the slope, snatching up a stone as she passed one. The wildcat leapt onto the unconscious Spartan and gashed him again with its claws, the pain of which snapped him back to his senses. Sweetbriar hurled the stone, striking the cat on the skull with such a jolt he was briefly blinded with concussion. And in that moment, Spartan placed his back legs under the cat and thrusting upwards launched him with enormous force high into the air. Still blinded by the pain from Sweetbriars stone, the cat failed to react by turning himself for landing and came down backwards against the broken wall. The impact was so great it broke his back instantly, and with his death the scarred one's desire for redemption in the eyes of Cleon ended. Not in glory, but as a lifeless raggedy cat stretched out across an old crumbling wall.

Sweetbriar ran over to the injured Spartan who was struggling, but failing to stand. She gently placed her little paws upon him

"Lie still brave wolf, your injuries are deep, and you must not aggravate them so" she said in a soothing voice "Your timely intervention saved my life, by what name should I thank such a noble wolf as yourself?"

"Sergeant Spartan at your service my lady, but it is I that must thank you, had your stone strike not come when it did that cat would've finished me. I saw you stand up against him as I approached, you may be a squirrel, but you have the heart and soul of a wolf".

As Spartan spoke, he coughed and his voice began to falter. Sweetbriar looked down at his chest and saw the hair stained with red. He took a heavy sigh and continued.

"And by what name should I address you, my lady?"

"Sweetbriar", she replied tearfully.

"Well Sweetbriar, your courage is an example to all, and I am honoured to have made your acquaintance. It has been a privilege to fight by your side, but for now I must rest".

And with those words Spartan closed his eyes and spoke no more.

Sweetbriar sobbed for this noble wolf she didn't know and now never would. Such is the cruelty of fate that it brought such a friend to her aid when needed most, only to snatch him away forever. But then, as if waking from a dream, Sweetbriar remembered the battle that still raged in the valley below, the outcome of which will determine whether it be friend or foe that next approaches.

There will be time enough for sorrow when this day is done, she told herself, we must rally what strength we have before another attack comes, and she made her way back up the slope towards the others. The last of the fighting was almost concluded as she arrived. The scouts were finishing off the last of the wildcats, while there were no surviving feral cats anywhere to be seen. Panic stricken, they had scattered in all directions except back towards Cleon and his army. Without the cruel leadership of the wildcats to whip them into battle they were free to go their separate ways and so they had seized on the opportunity and fled.

At the sight of Sweetbriar, Bramble came running to her and they immediately embraced with tears of joy at one another's safety. The wolves turned to look at her briefly before looking down towards where Spartan lay motionless. Without speaking they went to him and bowed their heads in silent sorrow before returning, and one of them addressed Sweetbriar.

"If you have somewhere safe you and your kin can escape to, we shall escort you there".

"We do, and it's not far from here" she replied, "Now come Bramble, we are not fully out of danger yet." And looking at the others, "All of you, help those you can, we can tend to our wounded once safely inside Frosthome".

With no further need for instruction the animals duly assembled. Sweetbriar remained by Bramble's side and Chindit limped along next to them. Trixie carried a wounded hare gently in her jaws while the other animals assisted those in need as best they could, and under the protection of their wolf escort they made their way up the field towards the forest and relative safety.

Passing through the tree line, the forest was serene and peaceful compared to the events of the day, and in a clearing ahead they saw the bank of Frosthome Hall, its welcoming entrance seemed to beckon them inside. With Fenrir and the other wolves remaining outside to stand guard, the rest of the party descended down through its main passage. Ignoring the many sub passageways that bisected it on they pressed until finally they reached the great chamber. And there laid out before them was the feast prepared for the day's festivities.

It seemed to Sweetbriar like a lifetime ago that they had left the comfort of Frosthome for the great party they had planned for the day. But these were no longer the happy carefree animals that had set out that very morning, the stress and horror of war had changed them greatly. They were now hardened by battle, some injured, but none broken. Sweetbriar wondered if life could ever be the way it used to be. The food will wait till the others return, she thought, for now we must prepare in case they do not.

While Chindit and the other casualties were made as comfortable as possible under the watchful eye of Trixie, Elderberry led the smallest of creatures deeper still into the safe dark tunnels of Frosthome. Sweetbriar headed back up to the entrance to join the wolves on watch.

Emerging into the sunlight she went to the nearest wolf and sat beside him.

"I am sorry for the loss of your friend; he saved my life at the cost of his own".

"No wolf wishes to fall in battle, but it is the price we are all prepared to pay for the privilege of service".

"You take your friends passing extremely well, I did not even know him, yet his death wounded my heart greatly".

"It is the tragedy of war that even the brightest of lights can be extinguished in an instant. Spartan was one such bright light and were it not for the cruel intervention of fate the light of his life would've burned brighter still. He was like a brother to me, we grew up in the rearguard together and his loss pains me greatly, but right now our duty is to the living. Later there shall be time to honour our fallen, but for now it must wait".

"Then I shall join you in honouring him. But I must ask, by what twist of fate brought you to our salvation, and from where have you come? To my knowledge there have been no wolves sighted in this area for many generations".

"We are scouts of a great company. Over many years our hunting campaigns have taken us in all directions, and this year the path we follow has led us here".

"Then you came here hunting cats?"

"We did not, nor did we come seeking battle either, but since battle is what we found, we could not simply sit back and watch you die. No, our hunt is for something else, something that was hidden long ago, and legend tells us that when we find it, hope shall be restored, for time heals all. Perhaps we seek hope, or maybe even time itself, we simply do not know for sure"

"But that doesn't make sense, surely neither hope nor time are objects to be found."

"It makes no sense to us either, but the trouble with legends is they are born from stories and like all stories they have a tendency to evolve with each retelling. How can we be sure the version we know today is even close to the original words of the first teller."

"What do you mean?" Sweetbriar enquired, eager to learn all she could.

"Well, let us imagine one day you are telling the tale of what happened here. You describe this valley as being formed from two spurs from that high peak yonder, but the person you tell this story to, imagines that peak as a mountain, so in their version of the tale that is what it becomes. The next listener imagines this great mountain is so high it's capped with snow. And so on and so on, until many generations from now your story is set beneath a foreboding, snowcapped mountain that pierces the clouds and is encircled by mighty eagles. Such incremental evolution is the unfortunate nature of all stories. Consequently, we can never be sure how much of them are original, or fanciful embellishments born from the imagination of later generations. If only we could find a way to somehow set our stories like stone so they never change, but the means to achieve such a notion is beyond the comprehension of this humble wolf."

Sweetbriar thought this over and was reminded of the human markings she had seen on so many artifacts.

"Perhaps the humans knew of such a way, for they left many marks and symbols on the relics they left behind. Could it be those marks tell human stories?"

"Maybe they do, but without the knowledge to understand them, those stories are lost to us. But please forgive me, I forgot my manners, I am Fenrir, by the way. That large she wolf over there is Athena, next to her, with the tip missing from one of her ears is Malkia. The young one with too much energy for his own good is Tuval. And then of course, there was Spartan, our beloved sergeant."

"Pleased to meet you Fenrir, I am Sweetbriar, but there's that word again, sergeant. I'd never heard the expression until Spartan addressed himself as such, what does it mean?"

"It is one of several designations of rank within our company that serve to denote levels of authority and responsibly. As sergeant, Spartan was the leader of our team, but his responsibility didn't die with him, as his corporal, it passed to me".

Sweetbriar listened with curiosity to this strange explanation. It seemed to her that Fenrir had described a completely different world from her own. A world in which fearsome wolves with strange names and ranks, guided by vague myths, hunt for something as elusive as time.

"Then you followed Spartan into battle because he commanded it?" she asked.

"No, he would not need to, we followed him because he was our friend".

This, Sweetbriar understood completely, these wolves with their strange words, names and ranks were not so different after all, friendship and loyalty were the guiding principles for her folk too.

Then Fenrir continued. "Now please Sweetbriar, you must go back inside and seal the entrance from within. Collapse it if you can, cats are not known for their tunnelling skills so you should be safe underground if they come".

"We shall not entomb ourselves in the dark while you face them alone, what can four wolves do against many? No, our place is up here facing whatever may come, together".

And then to Fenrir's amazement he saw more squirrels emerging from the entrance carrying as many small stones as their little arms could hold and began piling them high near the entrance, while other squirrels under Bramble's direction took them and scampered off into the surrounding trees.

"What is the meaning of this?" Fenrir enquired.

"We have already found a means to fight, and now we also have the advantage of terrain. Look around you Fenrir, we are in a forest, and we squirrels are masters of it."

Sweetbriar replied with determination.

27: THE GREY COMPANY

"Two armies meet for a fight, both are fearless and strong, but if one of them stands for what's right, then the other can only be wrong."

With Boudica leading the way, the company moved ever southwards through the woodland until they reached the base of a slope where she signalled them to halt, and in a low voice addressed Brasidas.

"At the top of this ridge you shall find Spartan and the others, and in the valley beyond a great battle is being fought, or at least it was when I left".

Brasidas instructed the company to remain in place while he and Darius would move up with Boudica to survey the situation from the ridgeline. Moving carefully, they were greeted by Uther who ushered them to stay low and join him with Ajax who was concealed in the undergrowth ahead.

"Where is Spartan and the rest of the team?" Brasidas asked.

"Tracking another party further along the ridge sir, though they've been gone a while now and still no word from them".

"I see, and what of the situation here?"

"There's a large army of cats attacking a line of badgers, foxes and dogs in the valley beyond the ridge. When we first arrived, the defenders were holding them off nicely but since Spartan left, their line began to fracture, and they've been forced to give ground. It seems they're trying to execute a fighting withdrawal to better positions but it's proving slow going. There's also an additional group of cats assembled down at the lower end of the valley, they may be a reserve that has yet to be deployed. But there's something else you should know sir, the enemy commander that is hanging around near the back of the fighting, it's Cleon."

"Cleon! I should've finished that wretch when I had the chance."

Moving closer to the ridge, Brasidas looked down into the

valley below and sure enough there was Cleon, the beast himself, and in a hushed tone Brasidas spoke to himself.

"I'll not seek the advice of a dead human vicar to tell me whose side I'm on".

"What was that sir?" enquired Darius who had come up behind him.

Without even answering the question, Brasidas turned and issued his orders.

"Bring the company up and have them form up in three ranks just over this ridge. I want you at the head of the left pack and when we pick up pace you are to break off to the left and lead them down the valley to intercept that reserve group. Don't get tangled in a prolonged fight, just keep them busy enough not to link up with Cleon's main force. I shall lead the other two packs straight down the slope into the flank of his army and if we can break them, we shall come to your aid and together we shall finish the job. Any questions?"

"What if you can't break them sir? You'll be greatly outnumbered, even if you had all three packs with you".

"To slay a serpent, you need only cut off its head, but if I cannot do that, then you'll find me in the poppy fields of Wolfhaven when your time comes".

Darius took one last look at the valley before turning about and returned to bring up the company. As he went Brasidas turned his attention to the three remaining scouts. "Follow the route Spartan took, but take care, the fact he and his party has not returned tells me some trouble befell them."

As Boudica and the others headed off, Brasidas stepped forward from the treeline onto the open ridge beyond and there he stood like a giant fell beast of legend, his eyes transfixed on the battle that raged below. The company began to emerge from the trees behind him and he heard a cry of concern from the closest of the defenders below as they thought they were about to be flanked, but his attention was firmly fixed on Cleon.

Dispersing from the tree line behind Brasidas the wolves formed up. Each pack, in three ranks deep, forming the left, centre and right wings of this fearsome company. And once formed in precise order, they stood rigidly awaiting their next command while Darius went forward to Brasidas and informed him the company was ready, but before departing to take up his own position ahead of the left wing he made one final comment.

"Wolfhaven can wait, I'll see you later, in this field sir."

For a few moments the company remained motionless for no order came. Brasidas stood silently, remembering his last encounter with Cleon. He had almost finished him then, but in his moment of triumph, he had seen Darius going down under many wildcats, so abandoning the opportunity and rushing to the aid of his friend, Cleon was able to escape the battle. Now Brasidas had the chance to finish what should've ended long ago. Then, with his attention turned back to the present, and without even turning to face the troops lined up behind him, he barked…

"Company will advance".

And on that, the whole formation began to march forward. Without a single paw out of step and maintaining their well drilled ranks, that grey mass of wolves moved down the slope with perfect precision.

"Double time".

With this second command the company quickened their pace but still maintained their formation. Darius and the left wing began to veer slightly left thus widening the gap between them and the centre, but still they went down the slope, closing the distance between them and their respective objectives as they went until finally, Brasidas issued the order they were all ready for…

"Charge".

With this, every wolf broke into full speed. Darius and the left pack broke off down the valley while the remainder under Brasidas went straight down to the battle below. Being careful to avoid the defenders, he led his packs just ahead of the defence line, and they crashed into the flank of Cleon's army with such force that many cats were trampled into the ground where they stood.

As Brasidas and the front ranks initial impact lessoned, the following rank passed through and smashed against more cats, then finally the third rank hammered the penetration deeper still. The cat's right flank reeled with disorder at this sudden change in fortunes. Witnessing this sudden and unexpected assistance, the morale boost it provided to Lord Hawthorn's beleaguered forces allowed them to fight with renewed vigour. Seizing the opportunity to rally his troops Hawthorne ordered the whole line forward, and they surged with all their might as they tried to break through the front body of cats to link up with that grey company of wolves they could see pushing deeper into Cleon's flank, and ever closer to Cleon himself.

Hawthorn knew nothing of Cleon, but he could clearly see that these wolves were fighting their way towards the largest of all the cats. Surmising that must be the enemy commander, he resolved to do the same. These wolves were unexpected but most welcome allies, Hawthorn thought, and if either force can bring down that big cat, then perhaps this battle can be won.

With the left of Hawthorn's line finding the fight easier now the cats had wolves to their rear, he quickly transferred a third of the badgers from the left to centre, thus strengthening it to hammer harder against the throng of cats to his immediate front. The added strength paid off and his line began to slowly take on an arrowhead formation as it drove a wedge deeper into the enemy front.

Brasidas and his packs were fighting tooth and claw for every inch of the ground between them and Cleon's position. The wildcats, like many creatures, were most ferocious when threatened and they fought like lions, and the closer the wolves got to Cleon, the stronger and larger the wildcats that defended him, his chosen ones, and most vicious of all, his personal guard.

The Wolves tore their way into them and in the bitter fighting many were wounded or killed but it was the wildcats and their feral minions that fared the worst. Except for the bodyguards and most senior of wildcats, they had been fighting all morning and their exhaustion was clearly having its toll on their ability to resist this sudden onslaught, and all the while the wolves of Brasidas and Hawthorn's badgers pressed ever deeper. Cleon could see the danger he faced but his arrogance would not permit retreat. He was determined even now that he and his army could still win the day, and he shrieked at them to fight harder.

Meanwhile, down in the eastern end of the valley Darius and his pack were closing in on the enemy reserves, but as they approached, they saw many of the cats simply flee in panic while the rest remained as they were either laying or seated on the ground. Darius had expected a fight but there was no sign of resistance at all. Getting closer he saw why. This was no mighty force held in reserve. Cleon had been so eager for victory he'd held nothing back and committed all his forces, and this was just the wounded remnants of earlier fighting. The bruised and battered cats that had suffered terrible injuries earlier that day and had retired down the valley to lick their wounds or die from them. Those that could still run had done so when Darius approached, and those either too injured to move or simply fed up with fighting were content to surrender and begged to be spared.

Leaving a team to guard the prisoners, not that they really needed guarding, content as they were to not be fighting anymore, Darius turned his two remaining teams about and led them back up the valley at great speed. He knew time was of the essence if he was to support Brasidas in his effort to bring down Cleon and drive his army from the field.

28: STANDING TO

Outside the entrance to Frosthome all was quiet. Alongside the four wolves, Sweetbriar and half a dozen of her squirrels stood waiting and watching. Just behind them in the entrance itself, Trixie and the uninjured hare acted as gate guards should anything get through the first line. As they all stood waiting and watching Bramble came scampering in from the trees to their front.

"Everything is ready" he reported as he caught his breath.

Sweetbriar smiled "Good, thank you Bramble, now please, get inside Frosthome where you will be safe. If these cats should come again mum and dad won't like it if they hear you put yourself in danger".

"I wish you all wouldn't keep saying that, I used to believe it but I'm not a child anymore. I'm old enough to understand mum and dad are dead. The whole idea that the morning after one of the worst storms in years they should suddenly decide to go away on a long trip without even saying goodbye to us is complete nonsense. I have understood that for a while now".

"Oh Bramble, I'm so sorry" Sweetbriar replied tearfully "You were so young, and we didn't want to upset you, but the longer we stuck to the story the harder it became to admit the truth, please forgive me".

"Of course I forgive you, I know why you did it but now that you understand I know the truth, you'll no longer use our parents as an excuse to keep me from staying up here with you. My place is by my beloved sister's side".

"Oh Bramble, our parents would be so proud of you, but you are still not yet fully grown, and if their spirits are looking down from the great canopy above then they would still wish for you to keep yourself safe. So please do as I ask and go down below, besides, we'll need someone down there to help with tending to the wounded".

Suddenly, Fenrir whispered for silence, someone approached. They all faced and scanned the forest for whoever or whatever it was. Slowly Sweetbriar raised her paw as if about to give a signal while the other squirrels stood ready to throw the stones they held. Silently they stood their ground, watching and waiting until finally, Fenrir sniffed the air and reassuringly bade them to relax.

"It's ok, these are friends approaching" he said as he stepped forward, and sure enough from the trees ahead came three more wolves. Fenrir went over to greet them and after a brief conversation he led them back towards Frosthome.

"These are more of our party, Boudica, Ajax and Uther, and you'll be pleased to know they bring good news. Our company has arrived and even now they join the fight in the valley below".

The relief this news brought to Sweetbriar was overwhelming, but Fenrir continued with a cautionary note.

"Our company is strong, but the enemy host is vast, even the combined might of both our forces will find victory a challenge".

Then Ajax spoke up, "Fenrir tells me you have injured amongst you, I am the medic of our team, and through our past engagements with cats we have gained some knowledge of treatment regarding claw wounds, so please, if you could kindly take me to them, I will see what I can do to help".

"Thank you Ajax, my brother Bramble here will escort you to them for as luck would have it he was on his way down there anyway, isn't that right Bramble?"

29: THE PRICE OF VICTORY

Cleon's options were growing limited with every passing moment, and while he still had the larger numbers, he lacked the ability to command them. Hawthorn's arrowhead was forcing open an ever-widening gap in his front, his right was collapsing as the grey company ploughed deeper into it, and while his cats fought ferociously, all Cleon could do from his position near the rear was scream angrily at those in ear shot to fight harder.

And then he saw him, Brasidas, fighting his way through the throng of battle and getting closer with every fallen wildcat. Cleon remembered this black wolf from their last encounter and any concern he had for his army's situation vanished from his mind. He had a score to settle, and he would relish the opportunity to do so.

Not waiting for Brasidas to reach him, Cleon began barging his way through his own troops to close the distance with his foe, until finally the two emerged into a form of clearing within the battle that raged around them.

"Time to settle this once and for all, Cleon, you escaped me once, but not this time" Brasidas growled.

Cleon's eyes narrowed with a sinister sense of satisfaction.

"You fool, you cannot even recognise your own weakness, and I escaped you because of it, you would value the lives of your own troops higher than the price of victory. I would never be so weak, I would sooner see all my forces perish than deny myself the sweet taste of blood".

And with that, the pair charged headlong at one another, Cleon leapt with his claws outstretched for the first strike, while Brasidas, keeping low, aimed for his underbelly. The pair collided in a clash of jaws and claws, and they tumbled into a snarling, hissing mass, as they each sought to overcome the other.

As their brutal combat raged, they were oblivious to all but their own personal duel, but just as Cleon thought he saw an opportunity for a lunge on Brasidas' unprotected rump, he failed to see the jaws that suddenly closed on his neck. Brasidas lifted Cleon clear off the ground and began shaking him this way and that. Cleon's mind grew dizzy and the world around him blurred, but then something unexpected happened.

A heavily wounded Lord Hawthorn came crashing through the ring of fighters around them and collapsed in a heap with four wildcats on his back attacking him with barbaric frenzy. The sight of this noble badger in such dire straits was too much for Brasidas to ignore and he instinctively released his grip on Cleon sending him somersaulting through the air like a rag doll and crashing to the ground amongst some of the dead cats that littered the area. As Brasidas ran to Lord Hawthorns' aid, Cleon slowly regained his senses.

Although his neck was bleeding and painful, he found himself still able to move. Keeping low to the ground so as to remain unnoticed amongst the dead and dying, he began to crawl through the throng of battle. If I can make my way to the rear, I can recover myself enough to come back and finish him, Cleon thought to himself.

Crawling through the last of the fighters around him, he reached the open field beyond. Safely away from the fighting and keeping low within the tussocks of long grass about the place, he turned back to face the battle.

"As long as you continue to show such empathy for your own, you will always be weaker than I. Next time it shall be me that inflicts the final wound and you shall not get the chance to….."

Those were Cleon's final words for in that instant he was dead. With his attention fixed firmly on the battle, he failed to see Darius and the other wolves charging up behind him. Low as he was to the ground the wolves didn't even notice Cleon as they trampled him into the turf when hurtling over his body to join the fight ahead. Much like his son before him, an insignificant end to an insignificant cat.

Whilst Brasidas was fighting off the wildcats that had been attacking Hawthorn, Delphine fought her way through and joined him. Together they fought off all comers, but something was slowly changing in the cat's ability to fight.

Although Cleon's death had gone unseen, his absence was starting to be noticed. His ruthless authority had been the glue that held his army together, without him, many in its ranks were becoming confused as to what they should be doing next. There was fighting in all directions, especially now that Darius' teams were attacking the rear of the army. The situation for the cats was critical and Brasidas knew it. He had one last card yet to play and now was the time to play it. Finding a brief gap in the fighting he looked up towards the northern ridge from where his initial charge had begun. Catching a glimpse of what he was looking for, he tilted his head up to the heavens and let out a long almighty howl.

From the trees on the ridge emerged a great number of wolves that formed a long thick line ready to attack. For a leaderless army on the brink of collapse the sight of another company of wolves about to join the battle would be enough to break even the most stalwart of souls. But in reality, this was not a true company of fighting wolves, but the rearguard of the old and young so formed as to ensure the largest were to the front to give the impression of strength. Though this deception mattered not, for there was something else, something that sent a shudder of fear through the hearts of every cat that dared to look. There, at the head of this apparent company was the fabled she wolf carrying her dead pup, her appearance on the battlefield was the portend of doom for any cat. Legend tells of her being present at the scene of every wolf victory since their first battle way back in the days of Cleon the 7th. How could she have lived for so many decades if not some immortal goddess of war, or more terrifying of all, a ghost.

With this apparition, the last vestige of the cats morale shattered and the army broke. The smaller cats fled the field in desperation, while many of the wildcats continued to resist, not to secure victory, but only to fight their way out of harm's way. While the vast majority headed down the valley a group of about two dozen chosen ones saw an opportunity to slip away unnoticed and headed up the valley towards the high forest. They hoped to link up with the scared one and his force that they believed were still sitting safely in the tree line. They could then escape through the forest together.

Cresting the hump in the slope they passed out of sight from the broken battlefield they left behind, a sense of relief washed over them, and they continued upwards towards the distant tree line. But their optimism was short lived when they came upon the body of the chosen one that still lay across the broken wall, and then the rest of their comrades that littered the ground further up. Knowing there was no point turning back they pressed on into the trees.

Slowing their pace slightly as they went through the silent claustrophobic woods, they felt uneasy as they sensed they were being watched. Finally, up ahead through the trees they saw a large badger set in a clearing, and in front of its entrance was a small line of tiny creatures. As they focused their eyes, they saw that these were merely half a dozen squirrels, so the wildcats advanced.

Sweetbriar slowly raised her paw, and her companions readied themselves, then in an instant she dropped her paw sharply while shouting "Fire". On this command, all the squirrels launched their volley of stones, but not just from those beside her, but also from up in the trees on either side of the wildcats. The cats found themselves pelted from all directions in a torrential downpour of stones so intense they didn't know what to do. Some tried running forward only to be beaten back by the hail of stones. There was no going back for more squirrels in the trees behind gave them a pelting. The flanks were the only option but that was soon ruled out when they saw on each side of them the wolves were waiting for any fool enough to try. If they stay where they are, they die, if they attempt to flee, they also die, their will to fight broke and there was nothing left for them but surrender. Hugging the ground closely, the cats put their paws over their heads and begged for mercy. And with that final act of submission, the last remnant of Cleon's once mighty army ended not with a roar but a whimper.

Seeing their pitiful state, Sweetbriar relented and ordered a cease fire, and while Fenrir and the other wolves secured the prisoners, she muttered softly to herself.

"There's been too much death this day, let it end now".

It was not long before she learnt that it had indeed ended when a small force of wolves under Darius guided by Delphine along with some of the badgers and foxes arrived. Overjoyed to see her friends, she ran to greet them.

"What news from the valley? Please tell me it's over".

"It certainly is" Delphine replied "we suffered many casualties but none more so than the enemy. Lord Hawthorn will tell you himself when he catches up. He refused to leave the field till the last of the wounded were tended to despite ignoring his own injuries. He'll no doubt be along shortly with the others".

While the animals of Greenvale caught up with one another, Darius went over to Fenrir who stood nearby.

"What is the situation here? We came across Spartan on the way up and I detailed some wolves to remain with him until we return."

Darius was deeply grieved by the death of Spartan for the pair had formed a close bond through the fate of Phineus, but he would not put grief before duty so listened intently as Fenrir briefed him on all that had transpired.

"You and your team have done well, now gather them together, we must return to the company. We have a battlefield to clear and prisoners to police before this day is done".

30: HONOUR THE FALLEN

Later that afternoon Lord Hawthorn and the rest of the valley folk returned. There were many injured amongst them, and they filed silently into Frosthome, their senses numbed by the horror of battle. They saw the food still laid out for the party, but few had an appetite for eating, content instead to simply slump on the floor and muddle through their conflicted thoughts. Juggling between the loss of so many friends and the relief of their own survival, for which some felt a measure of guilt.

Lord Hawthorn refused to rest despite the rigours of the day. His back was marked with many scars, but a badger's hide is thick, and he stubbornly dismissed them as mere scratches. His priority was not for himself, but the welfare of others. Once satisfied that those that needed help had received it and the rest were as comfortable as could be, he turned his attention to the situation they now found themselves in. Who were these wolves down in the valley, and what do they want here in Greenvale, he pondered. He summoned Delphine and Sweetbriar to join him as he walked outside.

"Come, let us walk down to where we have a view of the field below. Sweetbriar, while we walk, please brief me on all that happened up here, I already hear you faced the crisis well and proved yourself a stalwart leader. I wish to hear of everything that happened".

Lord Hawthorn listened quietly as Sweetbriar recounted all that had befallen her and her friends. Their desperate defence within a wall of hedgehogs, the use of stones as weapons and the intervention of Spartan and his scouts. As she finished, they had just arrived at the low ridge and from it they looked down into the valley. The wolves of the rearguard had set up a camp, while the others were busy with various duties.

"What are they doing?" Sweetbriar asked.

"While I was down there, their leader, by the name of Brasidas, along with half his force left to escort the prisoners far to the north with the intention of releasing them once far away from here. He left the one called Darius in charge of the field and it was he that bid me to join him in identifying the dead. Once we had done so, he then asked me if I wished our fallen to be honoured alongside his own. I did not understand what he meant but considering these wolves had saved us at great cost to their own I felt obliged to accept. Whereupon they proceeded to dig a long trench into which they carefully placed the fallen, both ours and theirs, before piling the earth back on top of them. I don't know why they bury the dead; we animals have never done so".

"Maybe we should" Sweetbriar interrupted "Every death is tragic, and seeing the remains of our dead succumb to the slow decay of time makes the pain all the worst. By burying their fallen, these wolves never have to see such things and can better remember their loved ones as they had lived."

"Putting it like that, I see your point Sweetbriar. It seems their way is more respectful than ours, and I agree, going forward perhaps we should do the same, though what they did next was a real mystery to me. One of them fetched some poppy stalks from lower down the valley and shook the heads of them over the freshly piled earth, scattering the seeds in the process. Interestingly they did not extend this courtesy to the many dead cats that litter the field. For those, they simply collected the bodies together and dumped them in several heaps about the place, and I can see from here that they continue to do so. But all this brings me to the matter I wished to discuss with you. There have been many old tales of wolves, bedtime stories mostly, but in all of them the wolves are portrayed as the villains. A cruel and aggressive species that hunt and kill for pleasure, yet from what I have seen of these wolves here, they are nothing of the kind. They look in every way like wolves, yet they don't behave very wolflike if you ask me. What are your thoughts on this Delphine, wolves are closely related to your kind, are they not?"

Delphine thought for a moment before responding.

"We were related in the ancient past when both wolf and dog lived in the wild, but we parted ways when my ancestors chose to connect with the humans. The wolves wanted nothing to do with us, and so they remained in that wild feral state. We also have stories of vicious wolves stalking the shadows in search of the unwary, but as you have said, these wolves do not match that fearful description. In fact, this may sound silly, but I would even go so far as to say these wolves seem almost human in their behaviour. As if they have somehow become the very race they shunned so long ago."

Hawthorn found Delphine's words interesting, and now turned his attention to Sweetbriar.

"You have spent some time with these wolves, what is your take on them?"

"I know little of cruel wolves from bedtime stories, but I can say that the ones I have met are noble, kind, honourable and brave. They are fiercely loyal and have a strong belief in duty. They have risked, and some lost, their lives for us. In our hour of need we could not wish for better friends than these. I know they have come here in search of something, though it is difficult to understand what exactly, for they do not know themselves. They seem to be trying to resolve some old legend or prophecy, and although they do not fully understand its meaning, only that somehow finding it will heal all. It is certainly not their intent to bring us harm."

This jogged Delphine's memory of something she had seen towards the end of the battle.

"Did you see her, the wolf that carried a dead puppy? Perhaps they hope to heal it, bring it back to life".

Hawthorn pondered this supposition before responding.

"I struggle to accept that these wolves, superstitious as they may be, would believe that they can resurrect the dead. If that was their intent, why would they go to such lengths to bury their own? No, there is something else here that as yet we do not fully understand, and as Sweetbriar put it, neither do they it seems. But for the time being at least, we are all of similar mind, these wolves pose no threat to us or our people, so for now, we can only wait until tomorrow when, I'm told by Darius, that Brasidas wishes to speak with us. So come, let us return to Frosthome and get what rest we can, it's been a long day."

With one last glance down at the busy wolves below, the trio turned and made their way back up the slope towards home.

It was almost dusk when Brasidas and his group returned to the valley. Their first act was to pay their silent respects at the grave of the fallen, but as they finished and came away, Brasidas looked across at the piles of dead cats and to his mind came the memory of the graves of enemy airmen that George had shown him in the cemetery. In death we are all equal, he thought to himself, we must respect not just our own. And so, walking over to the nearest heap he began to dig and as he did so the other wolves joined him. Together they dug a great crater, and into this they piled the remains of every cat that had died that day. So large was the number that the summit of this heap still stood a great height above the ground and the last cat to be placed at its very top was Cleon himself. Then they covered this with all the earth they had dug and once finished Brasidas addressed his company.

"Cleon dreamt of building himself an empire, so let this mound of death serve as his throne, and let it also serve as a warning against the cruel ambitions of other would be tyrants. From coast to sparkling coast these lands were once the dominion of our great king, and though he dwells now in Wolfhaven, our fealty to his memory endures. For above all things, he loved most the natural beauty of his cherished realm, and we shall unleash bloody war upon any that seek to usurp it. Now let our salute echo through the hallowed halls and poppy fields of Wolfhaven, so that our fallen friends and beloved king know we honour them so".

And with that, the entire company erupted into a mighty howl, even the pups in the rearguard joined in. A howl so loud that if it was heard in Wolfhaven none could say, but it certainly reached the animals in Frosthome and they were initially struck cold with fear. But Delphine reassured them for she knew this not to be a call of aggression but one of sorrow, and both her, and the rest of the faithfull joined in that great howl for they understood too well the grief of loss. And to this chorus of commemoration was joined the shrill cry of a mournful squirrel as Sweetbriar paid homage to the brave sergeant that had given his life for hers.

Then, with the howl drawing to a close, the wolves fell silent before that towering mound. Indeed, so great was its height that to this day, while the graves of the heroic defenders of Greenvale have long been lost to the ravages of time and the poppies that marked them have spread far and wide, that mound still stands tall as a silent testament to a great victory, and the gallantry of those that won it.

It was to be a long and restless night up at Frosthome, few if any of the animals could sleep. Their thoughts racing with unanswered questions. Who were these strange wolves that camped in the field below? For what purpose had they come? What did they want from us? All these questions and more tugged at their minds yet they must wait till the morning for the answers they so desperately wished for.

When morning finally arrived, so too did word that the wolves were on the move. Leaving their rearguard encamped in the field, Brasidas and the scout team under corporal Fenrir led the company up the slope towards Frosthome, and as they filed into the clearing outside its entrance, they wheeled to the left until Brasidas called them to a halt followed by a sharp right turn bringing them to face Frosthome, and there they remained, halted in the same formation of three ranks they had performed so smartly the day before. While the company waited, Brasidas, Darius and Kasandra took post front and centre, before they too came to a halt. There they remained, silently facing Lord Hawthorn, Delphine, Sweetbriar and the other animals that had emerged from Frosthome. Then, leaving Darius and Kasandra in position, Brasidas approached Hawthorn alone.

"I'm sure you have many questions, but first I think a more formal introduction is in order. I am captain Brasidas, back there is my second in command lieutenant Darius who you have already met, beside him is colour sergeant Kasandra, and behind them is our company".

The sight of Kasandra holding that dreadful thing in her

jaws filled him with horror but doing his best not to show fear Lord Hawthorn responded.

"Pleased to meet you captain, I am Lord Hawthorn of Frosthome Hall, this is Delphine of the faithful that have a community to the south of here. And this young squirrel by my side is Sweetbriar. But please sir, you are correct about us having many questions and we are most eager to ask them, but one most of all, what business brought you to this valley if not to save us in our hour of need?"

"The short answer to that is we were guided here by the gossip of a raven. A chance encounter with one last winter, and it told us of a strange valley in which he had witnessed different species working together as if one, but it was one particular detail of what this raven related that interested us so keenly."

Brasidas paused briefly, looking down at Elderberry who was a short distance back from Hawthorn, he then continued.

"The raven overheard a mole talking to some squirrels and badgers about a sealed door he had found deep below ground. If we have found the place of which the raven spoke then I ask you this, does this door remain sealed?"

"Indeed it does sir" Elderberry chipped in excitedly "do you have the means to open it?".

"I do not know, maybe or maybe not, we do not know for sure if this door of yours is the thing we are looking for. Having spent so many generations chasing dead ends, looking for anything sealed below ground, we've hunted through old mines, abandoned tunnels and damp caves, but as of yet, we have never found what we truly seek."

"And what is that?" Hawthorn enquired.

"In truth we do not know, only that it is of great importance, not only to us, but to the world as a whole. Perhaps to better explain our quest, I must first take you back to the beginning. A story that began over one hundred years ago and has grown in chapters with every new generation born into its hallowed pages. Only when this story is told, will you truly understand who and what we are, and armed with such knowledge, you shall better understand our purpose here".

31: THE BEGINNING

As the gate to the compound swung open the convoy rumbled through. Up the narrow concrete lane the vehicles went before pulling into the parking area adjacent to the HQ building. There, soldiers from the advance party had been assembled to assist with the unloading. As men jumped down from the trucks, others remained to pass down the many crates and bags they contained. From the lead vehicle, the company commander, major Carlyle, stepped out from the passenger side to supervise the work, while from its rear Seamus jumped down and surveyed their new surroundings.

Looking up at the high hills beyond the camp he saw a rugged grassy terrain, not green and lush as it should be, but sun scorched and yellowing. Where once many sheep would've grazed, now only a handful remained to nibble at the slim pickings the slopes provided. A far cry from London and Wellington Barracks, he thought to himself. There'll be no glorious parades here, just the dull monotony of guard duties. However, this was no military barracks, but a scientific research station. As the situation had deteriorated with harsh and unpredictable weather patterns plus the frequent power outages, various contingency plans had been made. So when the power failed completely these plans were triggered. With their advance parties already deployed, many different units headed out to their respective objectives. The scientists that worked in this quiet isolated backwater were considered an important national asset, and for this reason the company had been assigned to their protection.

"Move along Seamus, don't get under foot." came a voice from behind him. Seamus stepped aside as he looked round and saw corporal Smith with another guardsman carrying a large crate. "Run along and play with the others, there's a good fellow".

With his tail wagging, Seamus did as instructed and bounded over to the nearby grassy area where the other dogs were busy chasing and retrieving a blue ball that one of the handlers was throwing for them.

Although the youngest of all the dogs, Seamus was by far the largest. He was a huge Irish Wolfhound and had the honour of being the regimental mascot. A position for which he was immensely proud, more so because he had recently been commissioned with the honorary rank of captain by the king himself. He would often be seen on parade marching proudly at the head of the company in his glorious red cape, and the other dogs respected him greatly.

His friends were mostly the working dogs of the company. Firstly, there were the four guard dogs, all Alsatians, what they lacked in Seamus's height they made up for in muscle. Of these Sasha was the oldest and longest serving, then there was Saxon the strongest, plus the two new members to the team, brothers called Butch and Sundance. Next were the two sniffer dogs, both Black Labradors, Janey and Dutchess.

And lastly there was Freya, a Border Collie. Not interested in ball chasing as to do so she would need to abandon her own precious toy and that she'd never do. She was not one of the working dogs, though she often wished she was, and the others were very protective of her. She was the family pet of the company commander, and of all his family Freya loved most his young daughter Issabelle, who had sadly passed away from leukaemia some months ago. And since then, Freya had always carried Isabelle's favourite toy everywhere she went. It was a chocolate brown floppy cloth dog that was scented with a pouch of lavender concealed within.

Once the soldiers had finished unloading the trucks and settled into their new quarters, playtime for the dog's was over, now the real work would begin. Freya returned with her master to the HQ building, while Seamus and the others were led back down towards the gate and the kennels that were situated at the rear of the guardroom. Seamus was correct about the dull monotony of guard duties, more so for him as he had no role to fulfil. Sasha and the other guard dogs would take turns patrolling the perimeter, while Janey and Dutchess would help at the main gate ready to sniff around vehicles if any ever came, but none did. But poor Seamus had no duty to perform. With no parades to march on, he simply languished in his pen eagerly waiting to be let out for his twice daily exercise. The days turned to weeks and they in turn turned to months, and still there was no role for poor Seamus. At least Freya, from the comfort of her cushion at HQ got to see the comings and goings of the officers, and scientists that occasionally popped in from their compound at the rear of the camp. While she struggled to understand the complex discussions they held, she managed to grasp some of their meaning. The scientists seemed to be focussed mostly on plant life and how it was being impacted by the weather. Judging by their level of concern, she gathered the situation must be serious. Meanwhile the officers, her master included, were mostly worried about the power situation and dwindling supplies. They had been operating off their own emergency generators since their arrival which had proved a more reliable system than the intermittent failing grid they had been used to in London, but the fuel for it was not unlimited, so its usage needed to be rationed. And worst of all, winter was fast approaching, and they'd received no word from London on when the next supply run would arrive. In fact, there had been only broken and fractured radio chatter for a while, and when they finally had managed to get through the only response to their request was a simple "We're working on it, wait out." And that was the last message they ever received for the following day, not even the garbled broken chatter could be heard. All calls went unanswered, and the airwaves offered nothing but an eerie silence.

All the while Freya watched and listened, and each time the dogs would meet for their morning and afternoon exercise, she would share with the others what little she understood.

As winter set in, and since the whole purpose of their being there was to protect the scientists, it was deemed that if the supply of fuel for the generators runs low, then what remained in the vehicles should be syphoned out for use when the need arises. The research lab must remain powered for the work to continue. As long as they could get through the worst of winter, resupply must surely arrive soon. Canned food was plentiful, but the supply of bottled water was a different matter. As this ran low, they began supplementing it from a nearby stream that ran down from the hills above them. This could at least be boiled and purified to the best of their ability, and was initially used only for bathing, but later would eventually become their only source of drinking water.

For the first two months of winter this optimism kept them ever hopeful, and they never wavered from their commitment to the task at hand. They all knew their mission was of the utmost importance and there was no inconvenience that would inspire them to abandon it.

But just as it seemed perhaps, they had passed the halfway mark of a particularly harsh winter, a sickness began to take hold in the ranks of soldiers and scientists alike. They did not know from where it came or how it spread but its effect was brutal. Once infected, a victim would fall into a crippling sickness marked by fever and headaches, before finally losing the strength to even stand, let alone walk for any length of time. And the final phase would see the patient pass into a deep sleep before passing away.

The dogs watched on helplessly as the numbers at the camp dwindled. Whatever the affliction was that was attacking the humans so savagely, it had no effect on dogs. Then one day, Freya reported to the others that a small detachment of uninfected soldiers led by corporal Smith had been sent in search of fuel. A glimmer of optimism was restored. Isolated and cut off as they were, the camp had no idea of the fate of the world outside and had simply assumed it should be an easy enough task for a few healthy men to walk the ten miles to the nearest petrol station to get some fuel. It would be a hard slog carrying it back, but they were guardsmen after all, and hopefully they would also bring news of what was going on out there. The restoration of power should be well in hand by now, and the nation's doctors must surely be developing a cure for whatever this mystery disease is that is running rife through the ranks. Perhaps even now help is on its way, and news of it would be their salvation. But as the days passed and corporal Smiths party had still not returned that optimism rapidly waned, and all the while the death toll continued to rise.

Each day more graves were being dug, and still no help arrived. Then finally, two weeks after corporal Smith's departure, the last surviving dog handler came to the kennels.

"Ok Seamus, the commander has a task for you, and that includes the rest of you too, come with me".

As he swung open the gates of their pens, they bounded out excitedly. They all knew the way to headquarters and would've gladly run straight there but when they saw the slow pace at which the sickly handler moved, they chose instead to walk with him.

Once there, he led them straight inside and bid them to sit and stay. Freya was already there of course so they went over and seated themselves by her. Before them major Carlyle was in deep conversation with a few fellow soldiers of assorted rank and the science lady from the labs. Seamus had seen her occasionally before but never this close as she had always kept herself apart from the day to day running of the camp. Freya had seen her most often because as head of the scientific research team she had often attended the briefings that took place regularly at HQ, even if only as an observer.

She was a slight woman in her late forties with long dark hair. Seamus thought she was pretty for a human, while Freya just thought she always looked sad and alone, as if she longed for something she had long since lost but knew could never have again. But now she also looked weak and sickly, as did all the soldiers present. Whatever the illness was that was attacking the garrison, it attacked them too.

Finally, the major said to the others "Ok then, we are all in agreement, this is the only way", the others nodded and the science lady handed him a small rectangular card like object which he proceeded to place in a small flat case which he snapped shut with a click. He then turned to face Seamus and his friends.

One of the other officers then spoke, "How will they carry it, should we strap it to one of them?" he asked.

The major ponded this for a moment before answering.

"No, if whichever dog it's strapped to should fall, the

others would simply carry on without it, then it would be lost forever. No, I have a better idea, Freya, give me your toy".

Obediently Freya released her beloved toy from her mouth and allowed her master to take it, though it pained her to do so. Alerted by her distress the other dogs stood and watched on with concern.

"See how it upsets her so to be parted from her toy, and also see how alert the others have become to her distress. She handed it over freely because she knows me, but had some stranger tried to take it, I'm sure the others would've done all they could to secure its safe return."

Then turning the toy in his hands, he pulled open the velcro fastener that secured the compartment in its belly and removed the pouch of lavender from within. This pouch was sealed with a draw string which he carefully loosened before pouring out some of the seeds. Once he had made enough space, he slid into it the small plastic case before resealing it. And with the pouch placed back inside the toy, he handed it to Freya which she happily received, and the others relaxed once more.

"Now then, the task I have for you is simple. We are too sick to travel with you, but the package Freya carries must get to London at all costs. It is of the utmost importance that its contents get to Wellington Barracks and delivered into safe keeping. They shall know how to keep it safe until the time comes to open it. As captain, you Seamus shall be in command. Sasha, as the oldest and longest serving, you are to assist Seamus in his duty, and the rest of you shall follow their lead. Now, be vigilant out there, stay off the roads where you can, and avoid towns and villages along the way as we don't know the dangers you may face, and bear in mind, a hungry human would sooner eat a dog than pet it so trust no one until you get home to Wellington Barracks. Just remember, soldiers good, everyone else bad."

With the company commander's brief instruction over one of the other officers then interjected. "You're certain they understand sir, no matter how intelligent they may be, they're still only dogs?"

"Don't underestimate them, our words may mean little to them, but I'm convinced they understand the meaning of what we speak. Isn't that right Seamus?"

On hearing his name, Seamus barked with acknowledgement.

"Well, I hope for all our sakes that you are correct major. The last hope for our world is riding on your faith in these eight canine companions.

He was correct, Seamus and the others did understand for the most part. They had to get whatever this thing was to Wellington Barracks at all costs, and trust nobody along the way.

The science lady then kneeled before Seamus and placed her hand gently on his head. And with a sorrow in her eyes that until now he had not noticed, though Freya had, she spoke to him.

"Go with grace gallant captain, and do not let your love for us stay you from your course, for should you return, you shall find nothing here but death. Your only way is forward, so I bid you farewell."

And with a last gentle rub to his head, she stood again and dressed back with the other soldiers. Major Carlyle then continued.

"Freya, I know you do not wish to leave me but if there was another option I would've taken it. No, this is the only thing left we can do. But worry not for me, soon I shall be going to join Issabelle in a place where dreams never end, and when you finally reach the end of a long and happy life, you can join us too, but not yet. For now you must go with Seamus and the others, complete this task I have given you, and once done, live your life to the full. Farewell my sweet Freya." and after tearfully kissing the top of her head he turned his attention towards Seamus, "You have your orders captain, dismissed".

And with no more words, he and the other soldiers brought themselves to attention and saluted.

Seamus knew what this meant and solemnly led his team, including Freya, out through the open doorway and back into the frosty morning air. There they paused briefly, looking at the vehicles that had brought them to this place so long ago. Then over at the makeshift cemetery that dominated the nearby lawn. It seemed like another world in which they had played so happily on that grass, but Seamus knew playtime was over. As he looked up at the grey clouds above, watching him do so, Shasha spoke.

"It won't come, it never does anymore" she said.

"What won't come?"

"Spring" She replied, "There'll be no sunny strolls through daffodils for us, just dark skies, torrential rain and a ponderous slog through a sea of mud. Enjoy this frost while it lasts".

With no further words Seamus led them down the narrow lane towards the waiting gate guard, while a short line of guardsmen saluted as they passed. Seamus ran the task he had been handed over in his head. It all happened so quickly, one minute he was languishing in his kennel with no job to do, the next minute he's commanding a mission of the utmost importance. Can he live up to the enormous responsibility he'd been entrusted with. He was determined to prove he could, after all, he held the Kings commission, and the honour of his species was at stake. He would not be the dog that failed in his duty.

Passing through the gate into the lane beyond they paused again briefly, but unwilling to look back, they proceeded. Initially keeping to the lane for a short while before branching off as instructed. They had no reason to follow it for it headed east, before eventually disappearing into a forest, and although it was the route by which their vehicles had originally come, they had no knowledge of road signs or maps by which to navigate. They only knew that London and their home at Wellington Barracks lay somewhere in a generally southern direction.

It was to prove slow going, for their route took them across rolling hilly terrain with little cover. Doing their best to avoid the occasional silent farmhouses that dotted the land. Their only concealment from these were the stone walls that crossed the land here and there, but using them would often force them on long wide detours from their desired course. Larger settlements took longer to work their way around, but even these were quiet and seemed devoid of life, apart from the crows that could often be seen circling above them.

On the third day they came upon a river but its only crossing point via a bridge would take them dangerously close to a building. It was here they learned the fate of corporal Smith's team, but as for him, they found no trace, neither there, nor anywhere else along their journey.

Releasing sporadic showers, the cloud had darkened with each day until the fifth when the heavens opened with a vengeance and Sasha's prediction was unleashed upon them. A torrential rain so hard they were forced to take what shelter they could get beneath an old, rusted farm trailer they found abandoned in the corner of a field. Cold and soaking wet, a whole day was lost under this barely adequate shelter as they huddled together for what little warmth they could muster.

The next morning the rain continued but had lessoned slightly so Seamus decided they should carry on regardless. Trudging through the sodden fields and traversing swollen streams, on they went, ever southwards. Days and nights rolled by, and they lost count of how long they had travelled as they weaved their way down the country, but they did notice the change of scenery as they went. The high hills had receded to a flatter fertile land. Towns and villages became both larger and more numerous. Roads were more dominant features with wide lanes and often bordered by high banks, though no traffic moved along them. The world the team walked through was silent and devoid of all movement apart from themselves and the other wildlife they saw along the way. The only thing that broke that eerie silence was the rumbling of thunder each time another storm descended upon them.

But the biggest challenge they needed to overcome was hunger. The morning of their departure they had been fed a larger than usual breakfast of dog biscuits with the added bonus of some sausages from the cook house. But since then, they had needed to forage for every morsel. There were no biscuits to be found anywhere, let alone sausages. They tried their best to eat whatever they saw other animals eating with mixed results. Half a dozen earthworms may be a feast to a robin, but to a dog, was little more than a rather unsavoury snack. There were no nuts or fruits to be had this time of year, so their main source of food were the mushrooms that thrived in the damp decaying conditions of this deserted world. While not so tasty as the treats they had long been accustomed to, these were enough to sustain them, so on they went.

It was to take them nearly two months of wandering this way and that before they finally came to the last rural spot before the edge of London itself, an old, ruined barn nestled in some overgrown scrubland. It lay in the lee of a large road junction that bordered the suburbs of the great city. Beyond this point there would be no further sneaking around the edges of settlements, they would need to enter this urban sprawl to reach their objective. Seamus decided they would rest for the night in this neglected spot before pushing on at first light. So, finding what comfort they could on the rough ground, and taking turns at watch, they hunkered down to a restless night under the stars.

With the arrival of dawn, they broke cover of the scrub and headed up the embankment to the junction. The road was still as eerily quiet as it had been all night. No vehicles could be heard in any direction, and the few they saw along the road were empty and abandoned. But on the far side of the road the bank sank down again into a retail park, and the entire site was filled with many military vehicles, ambulances and large tents. Seamus had seen these before, it was an emergency field hospital. Feeling reassured by the hope of finding more soldiers, the team moved in, but that hope soon dissolved as they did so. The smell of death hung heavy in the air, the only sign of life was the multitude of rats that scurried in and out of the tents, and flies buzzed everywhere. Ambulance doors were open and on some of their gurneys lay the decomposing remains of the patients they had brought to this forlorn place. The main hospital tents were even worse, so rancid and choking was the smell from their entrances, the team could not bring themselves to even enter. It was now painfully clear that whatever sickness had struck the garrison, had cast its grim shadow far and wide, and had done so long before it had reached their lonely outpost.

Leaving that place of death they continued on their way, pressing ever deeper into the suburbs. The roads were lined with silent buildings and houses, their windows dark and lifeless, and in many places along the pavements were piled many bodies. Some placed carefully in bags for collection, while others were either dumped less ceremoniously, or lay where they apparently fell. It seemed that at some point an effort had been made to control the situation, but as the fatality rate grew, and the dead outnumbered the living it simply became impossible to manage, and death claimed them all. Here they saw not only rats, but cats could be seen on every corner, every wall, and down every alley. Being able to leave their homes at will they had thrived off the abundance of hunting opportunities on these rat-infested streets. The deeper they went into London, the more this scene was repeated. The towering buildings of that great metropolis now stood dark and empty; the whole city had become a mausoleum to the age of man.

Hardening their resolve against the pitiful sights before them, they marched through this city of the dead until finally, they arrived before the open and unguarded gates of Wellington Barracks, headquarters to all the proud regiments of the royal guard. They were home at last, and soon their mission would be complete. With pride in their achievement, they passed through the gates onto the forecourt beyond, now they need only find an officer and deliver Freyas sacred cargo. Entering the large doors to the barracks they were greeted by empty silence. Papers and boxes lay strewn across the floor of the many offices within, but all hope was lost when they finally reached the Guards Chapel. It was here they discovered the fate of their beloved guardsmen. That magnificent and venerated hall of the household division where once soldiers, veterans and civilians alike would gather in peaceful prayer or glorious song, now served only as a silent morgue. With a heavy heart, Seamus, without speaking, turned about and left, the others slowly followed. Crossing the road outside they entered St James Park and dejectedly slumped themselves down on the now neglected and unkempt lawn.

There they sat, lost in their own thoughts until finally Seamus broke the silence.

"Well, that's it then, we've failed. To have come all this way only to find it has been for nothing."

"We haven't failed, we made it to Wellington Barracks as ordered and the package remains safe in our possession" Sasha replied.

"The package may be safe but what use is it to us? Seamus retorted, "Our orders were to deliver it into safe keeping but there's nobody left alive to receive it, they're all dead".

And with that Seamus slumped even lower into a state of deep depression. Freya watched and could keep silent no longer, angered by his surrender, she snapped.

"Pull yourself together captain, we haven't failed at all. We were tasked with delivering the package into safe keeping and that is exactly what we have done, it's safe in our keeping. So stop moping about like a lost lamb and buck your ideas up. Remember who and what you are, you are an officer in the British army".

"I am not a proper officer, I'm a dog, it's just an honorary rank, and even if it wasn't, what difference would it make, there is no British army, everyone is dead".

"I will not hear any more of this defeatist nonsense, did corporal Smith throw in the towel? No, he took up those empty cans and carried on".

"And what good did it do him?" Seamus replied gruffly, "We know he didn't make it back with any fuel, for if he had done, they would've driven here ahead of us".

This annoyed Freya even further, and she responded sharply.

"Maybe he died trying, but at least he didn't give up. Now pull yourself together and get a grip of the situation. You may hold an honorary rank, but you are the only officer we have. Perhaps the last living creature on this earth to hold the kings commission, so start behaving like it. We seven, and I include myself in this, are your army, accept your responsibility captain and lead us".

Shamed by Freya's rebuke, Seamus regained his composure.

"I wish it were that simple Freya, but how can we be real soldiers without training?"

"You shall train us Seamus. My master used to say that all the drills performed on parade, used to be how soldiers moved and fought on the battlefield in the olden days. You already know these drills and parade formations, also the traditions, ranks and battle honours of the army. Sasha and her crew already know how to guard and attack if need be. Dutchess and Janey are excellent sniffers and can search for anything. All we lack is military training and discipline, so teach us, mould us into actual soldiers."

Seamus took this in thoughtfully, then rising with resolve he slowly yet silently looked each of the companions in the eyes. Then after a brief pause, he addressed the group.

"Freya has reminded me of my duty, and in so doing she has also highlighted the fact we all still have a duty to perform. We may be small in number, but we are the last of his majesties soldiers and as such it falls to us to complete the mission before us. Now we just need to figure out what that mission is. That item Freya carries is of great importance, what was it they said? It shall be kept safe until the time comes to open it, open what? Whatever it is, they believed it to be the last hope for the world. Freya, you were in the meeting room before we arrived, did you hear anything else they discussed?"

Freya cast her mind back to that fateful morning, trying to visualise herself in the room. There was a heated discussion between the soldiers and the science lady, the words and phrases meant little to Freya but then she remembered, towards the end of the discussion the science lady said something that seemed to finally settle the discussion.

"Everything is safely sealed below. Our only hope now lies in time, for time heals all, time without us".

Freya recounted this but what did the science lady mean, hope lies in time, and time heals all? And why did she add, time without us.

Seamus and his companions sat in silence as they pondered whatever it meant, it was clearly of great importance to the humans. Sasha then broke the silence.

"So the item we seek is time, and when we find it, the thing Freya carries will open it and all will be healed. Perhaps it will heal all the humans".

Dutchess then joined in, "If time has a scent, Janey and I will find it, though perhaps not in this city of the dead for here the stench of death masks all else".

Seamus was unwilling to accept such a ridiculously simple explanation.

"Nothing can heal the dead, besides, how can we find time, let alone open it. There must be something we are missing. All we really know is the item they placed inside Freya's toy could be used to open something, but we don't know what. With such scant information to go on, all we can do is search for anything that is sealed and try our best to open it, but that would mean searching every single building, and trying to open every door, crate, box and cupboard in the world, that would be impossible."

"Not quite". Came a gruff voice from behind Seamus.

Seamus spun round in surprise and there behind him stood an enormous wolf. The companions leapt up defensively at the appearance of this formidable looking creature, but as they did so, several more wolves slowly emerged from the surrounding bushes, and they found themselves encircled. With an authoritative air, Seamus addressed the large wolf that had spoken first.

"I am captain Seamus of the Irish Guards, who are you and what is the meaning of this intrusion into our business?"

"My name is Leonidas, for that is the name the humans gave me. I am the Alpha of this humble pack. As for the meaning of our intrusion, you claimed your search impossible, yet you forgot the other thing Freya said. Everything is safely sealed below. So what you seek is not in houses above ground but somewhere below it. Admittedly still a difficult search but at least it's narrowed down a bit."

Freya was startled that Leonidas called her by name.

"How do you know my name sir, have we met?"

"We picked up your trail three days ago and have been tracking you ever since. We have kept our presence secret, but we have remained close enough to watch, listen, and above all, learn everything we can about all of you".

"And why would you do that?" Seamus asked, feeling a little embarrassed that they hadn't noticed these wolves until they chose to make their presence known.

"At first, we were just curious as to where you were going and why. You seemed to be so determined to get somewhere, we thought it might be worth our going too. But as we learnt more about you, we became more intrigued, and having heard just now about you being soldiers from an army, we want to join too. We managed to stay on your trail unseen for three days, our skills with stealth and hunting should prove very handy in your quest. What do you say captain, please let us join."

"But why would a pack of wild wolves seek the discipline of army life?"

"Because despite our appearance we are anything but wild. We were born and raised in captivity at Hertfordshire Zoo. Neither we, nor our parents and grandparents have ever been truly wild, we know only the routine and order of zoo life. When the collapse came, and the visitors stopped coming we would've perished within our compound were it not for the kindness of one of our human keepers. Despite the chaos outside he did his best to feed us, until even that became impossible for him. And at the end, when he accepted his world was lost, he opened the gates to our compound and set us free. But what is freedom without purpose? We knew nothing of the outside world, and it seemed to us that we were condemned to simply wander aimlessly until death claims us for the final trek to Wolfhaven. But just when all hope had abandoned us, we stumbled upon your trail. Your talk of duty was music to our ears, this army of yours is precisely what we need. We shall be your soldiers, and we shall have routine and purpose again."

"Sorry to interrupt but what is Wolfhaven?" Freya enquired.

"It is the place we go to when we die".

"Is it where dreams never end?"

"Well, I guess it must be, because none have ever returned".

"Then that is where my master and Issabelle are waiting for me when my time comes".

"And may that be a long time coming young Freya, there's no rush to open that particular door". Leonidas said softly with a smile, then turning back to Seamus "So what do you say captain, will you accept our offer of enlistment into your army?"

"I do," Seamus replied promptly "but if we're going to do this, we must do it right. We all have a mix of skills that we can bring together and share with one another. Although small in number, we shall style ourselves as a company. As captain I shall act as company commander and be responsible for all things military related. You Leonidas shall serve as my second in command and for that I appoint you to the rank of 1st lieutenant. We shall divide the remainder into two platoons with an equal number of wolves and dogs in each. I shall appoint Sasha to the rank of 2nd lieutenant to command one of the platoons while you Leonidas shall chose your best wolf to command the other. Who shall it be?"

"Then I chose Persephone, she is able and strong, but above all, wise".

"Then I hereby promote her to the rank of 2nd lieutenant. Ok then, that leaves only one more appointment. Freya caries the very thing we must all vow to protect with our lives, and in recognition of her sacred duty, I hereby promote her to the rank of colour seargent effective immediately. Ok then, any questions?"

"Actually, I have one" replied Leonidas "What's a platoon?"

"It's a smaller team within a company, think of it like you would a pack".

"Then can't we just call them packs instead? It would

make a lot more sense to us wolves".

"Ordinarily I would say certainly not, but in light of the fact that you are new to army terminology, then on this occasion ok, packs they shall be."

And so it was, on a cold afternoon in St James park the last company of the Irish Guards assembled, and with captain Seamus at their head, the long hunt began. Their first objective was the dark and silent tunnels of the London underground. Where better place to hide something below ground than in a forgotten corner of an old, abandoned tunnel. So tirelessly, and meticulously they spent much of the remaining year searching every twist and turn of each line, but all to no avail. Whenever they resurfaced to rest, eat and plan between searches, they would drill and train in the steadily overgrowing parks and gardens of the city above. And once ready, would always return below to continue the search, though each time they did so the water levels below were noticeably higher. The tunnels were slowly flooding and without human intervention there were no pumps to prevent it. But fortunately, by the time they became impassable, Seamus and the company had already concluded that what they seek lies elsewhere. And so, they marched out into the world in search of new tunnels, holes and caves to find and explore.

As one year turned to two, the bond between them was so firmly formed they became a great extended family and many of them found mates and had pups to add to the ranks of the ever-growing company. All the young ones were trained from birth in the duties of soldiering. Constant drills and lessons in the rearguard saw to it that when they came of age, they were more than ready to join the great hunt and continue the mission. Although there was no longer a human king, every pup to come of age would swear an oath of loyalty to his memory. As his guardsmen they swore to protect his lands, its people, and to restore hope to his beloved realm. In time Seamus, Leonidas, and all the others passed over to Wolfhaven, yet their descendants had learnt every lesson, and the company grew ever stronger. The teachings of Seamus consisted of far more than drill, history and custom alone, for he had lived his life in the barracks and encountered soldiers only while they were on duty. He had never experienced the mischief off duty soldiers can sometimes get up to. He knew nothing of the outside world beyond the confines of the barracks or parade grounds. The machinations of politics, corruption of greed or wealth, no jealousy or ruthless ambition. He knew only the blessed virtues as he perceived them, duty, honour, courage and self-sacrifice. These were the lessons he handed down to the company, and while he could never have known it, in doing so he had created a company of soldiers far more noble and virtuous than any human army that went before. As the company grew in numbers, more non-commissioned ranks were added to command the multitude of smaller teams that made up the packs. From this pool of dependable and skillful NCOs new officers would be promoted to fill the roles left by death or retirement. Freya's role as colour sergeant passed over to another, and then another, down through the generations, and all the while her precious cargo remained guarded and safe. With each generation the genes blended further, the company became more wolflike in appearance and size, retaining the keen night vision and hunting prowess of the wolves, yet always tempered with the discipline, duty and loyalty of the dogs. Years became decades, and still they searched. The lands around them changed, human buildings either crumbled and fell or were swallowed up by weeds or floodwater. Eventually the great storms and extreme weather that had plagued the world slowly diminished, and it seemed the seasons were returning. But much remained missing from the land, so food was always scarce. Times of strife would come and go, the company would always defend the innocent creatures of the land against those that sought them harm. Many noble deeds were done, great battles were fought, and countless lives saved. Yet these diversions and countless others were all deemed as inconvenient obstacles to the true quest. Until concluded, there has been, and always shall be, only the hunt.

32: LEGACY OF MAN

As Brasidas brought the story up to the present day, he paused briefly to allow his audience time for thought, before he proceeded.

"And there you have it, our story is told, and here before you stands the proud descendants of Seamus and his companions, both dog and wolf alike. The last company of the Irish Guards, proud soldiers of his late Majesty, and ardent defenders of his sacred realm. Now please, Lord Hawthorn, you have a door to show us, and I'm sure you now understand how eager we are to see it."

Lord Hawthorn looked again at colour sergeant Kasandra and realised the thing she carried was not a dead puppy, but a weather worn and raggedy old toy.

"Of course captain, it would be our honour to show you, please follow us, we shall take you to it immediately".

It was a small party that set out for the door. Lord Hawthorn led the way accompanied at his side by captain Brasidas. Sweetbriar and Elderberry gained a ride on Delphine's back while Darius and Kasandra followed at the rear. Passing through the forest they proceeded uphill towards the young trees ahead. Passing one of the old ruins that Elderberry used to house his collection of artifacts and not much farther beyond this they reached the entrance to the tunnel. Descending this they finally came to a halt before Elderberry's now famous sealed door.

Brasidas stepped forward and examined it closely. Taking his time before stepping back to address the others.

"In all the long years of searching, the company has never encountered anything like this. Its uniqueness makes me all the more convinced we have finally found what we are looking for. Colour sergeant, please step forward and present your burden".

Kasandra did as instructed, and at the foot of the door she placed the ragged remains of Freya's toy, before stepping back.

"Well, what happens now?" Elderberry enquired after a

brief silence. "How does this open the door?"

"This doesn't, its what's inside it that might" Brasidas replied.

"And what exactly is inside it?" Sweetbriar then asked eagerly.

"We do not know for we have never seen it, but we believe it to be some kind of key. The item was placed within by the nimble fingers of human hands, but I fear we would only destroy it, were we to try to remove it with our jaws. However, perhaps the dextrous paws of a squirrel would prove more than capable of retrieving it safely, would you care to try young Sweetbriar?"

Gingerly stepping forward, she carefully examined the toy before picking it up and turning it over in her paws. Sure enough on its belly ran a seam held together by some strange rough fabric. She gently hooked her paws between it and as she began to tug, it made a strange creaking noise as it separated. Inside was an old stained bag fastened by a frayed and tattered cord. This she opened with ease and within its contents of dried dead seeds she found a small flat case which she carefully slid free and turned over and over as she scanned every detail of it. On one side she saw two tiny hinges and on the opposite side a small button. Pressing this, there was a slight click and the case popped open.

The others gathered round eagerly to see what was within, and she held it up for all to see. A single flat rectangle of some unknown material. It bore no markings but for at one end could be seen a tiny symbol comprised of four curved lines that decreased in size.

"What on earth is it?" Lord Hawthorn asked disappointedly.

"I'm not sure, but I've seen this symbol before, up there on that little shelf thing, it must be connected somehow. If someone could help me up there, I'll see if I can figure it out".

Brasidas offered immediately. "Here, climb on my head and I'll lift you up", and as he bent low Sweetbriar scampered onto the crown of his great head and he lifted her high up the wall. Once level with the box and its little shelf she was lost as to what next to do. There was nowhere into which this flat card would slide, just the same matching symbol displayed on both card and shelf. What on earth could it mean. These were clearly connected but how. Then, as if from nowhere it popped into her head. Of course, it's so simple, they are connected, I just need to connect them. She placed the card flat onto the shelf and in that moment, there was a quick beep, and the little red light turned green. Quickly getting down they all backed away slightly as they heard a series of faint clicking sounds from within. This was followed by a brief pause before suddenly the door made a hissing sound and released a great gust of cold air from around its seal. Then it began to swing slowly inwards, accompanied by that mechanical clicking sound until finally it came to a silent halt, and beyond it, all was dark and cold.

As they stood, straining their eyes into the darkness, a sudden buzzing noise was heard from way up the tunnel behind them. They swung round in surprise and to their amazement, the furthest wall light back at the entrance began to flicker into life. After a couple of stuttering flashes it burst into radiant light, and this was then followed by the next, then the next. One by one the lights came on along the passage towards them. They had never in their lives witnessed such human magic at work, and they were struck with awe.

When this advance of illumination reached them, it did not stop at the door but continued through, and before their very eyes that dark void beyond burst into glorious light. They found themselves looking into a large chamber filled with many rows of racking shelves, and on these were countless containers of varying size and shape. Some cylindrical, others squarer like crates, but all of them neatly positioned and untouched since the day they were placed there by human hands.

Silently stepping into this room, they looked about themselves in wonder. Darius was the first to break the silence.

"What is this place? Impressive it may be, but how can these containers hold the hope of the world?"

Brasidas had no idea, but as he looked ahead, he spotted a

tiny red light displayed on another small shelf next to a large black panel on the far wall of the room.

"Sweetbriar, bring the card you carry, let's try it on that one too".

As Brasidas got close to the wall, she leapt onto his back and ran up to the top of his head. Repeating the process with the door, she placed the card flat on the shelf and the light instantly turned green. She leapt down and they all stood back expecting either the panel or perhaps even the whole wall to somehow open, but what happened next was far more magical than they could ever have imagined.

The black panel went from black to bright light and there before them was the image of a human seated behind a desk but facing them directly, but this was no still image, she moved and to their amazement she spoke to them. And what was even more amazing, the wolves and Delphine understood her, as if some ancient knowledge that had lain dormant in their minds had been suddenly triggered by the activation of this screen. And, here they were, facing a human as she had lived, and hearing her actual spoken words as she addressed them. They were mesmerized by her, Brasidas most of all. He took in every detail of her face, how her hair hung, how her eyes sparkled yet within them there was sorrow, and how her lips moved as she spoke. And when she did so, her voice was like that of an angel to his ears.

"My name is Doctor Helen Fisher, if you are watching this and all has gone to plan then I am long dead. But do not mourn for me, for I chose this lonely life of science from an early age. I dedicated myself completely to the pursuit of knowledge at the expense of all else. There is no family to miss my passing, nor a cosy homestead awaiting my return. I've spent my life moving from one soulless bedsit to another for the sake of my work. And now my journey ends here in this isolated facility. No, spare your pity for my colleagues and the soldiers that protect us. For they have left their cherished families for the sake of this duty and will perish separated from those they love so dearly. Now, as for this duty, we had hoped to somehow find a way to help our many plants survive the harsh and extreme weather patterns that are aggressively attacking our world. Unfortunately, we failed, there is no substitute for light and water in the correct quantities. Our seasons are disappearing, and I fear that with them many of our plant species will follow, so we are left with only one hope. Here in this vault, we have gathered the seeds for every plant that ever grew in this once fertile land. The fact you have now decided the time is right to open the vault then I trust the world has healed enough for them to grow once more. This precious store of life I pass to you, and with them also I offer an apology, I am truly sorry for all the damage we did to the world. These seeds I pass to you with hope, not hope for ourselves, for we are already dead, no, hope for you, whoever, or whatever you are, and hope for the world you have inherited. Now I shall bid you farewell but leave you with a warning. This facility has been ticking over on a trickle charge from its batteries to keep it cool and airtight, once activated the power levels will have spiked and have begun draining what power remains far faster. Depending on how long it has been since first sealed, you could have anywhere between a few days to a few weeks before the power is gone completely, and when that happens some of the vault's contents will begin to spoil. So you must waste no further time, save what you can, and save our beloved world. Farewell, and once again, I am sorry".

And with that, the screen returned to black, and she was gone.

At first the animals stood in complete silence, still trying to comprehend what had just happened, then finally Hawthorn's voice broke the spell "What on earth was all that funny noise about?"

"That funny noise as you put it was the language of the humans" Delphine replied, "And although I cannot explain how, I understood every word she said".

"So did I" Darius responded though equally confused as to how, while Kasandra agreed that she had too. "Captain, what do you make of all this?"

Brasidas still remained silent, staring at the now blank

screen oblivious to the question.

"Captain, sir, are you alright?" Darius enquired with concern.

Then Brasidas slowly turned to face them. "You heard the lady, time is precious if we are to save the contents of this place. Lord Hawthorn, these containers hold the seeds of life. All the fruits, nuts and grains you could ever imagine can be grown from these, and it falls to you and your people to make good use of them. We have finally found what we were for so long hunting, hope, and that hope I hand to you, use it wisely. And now our work here is done".

And with no further words Brasidas walked back out of the chamber and up the sloping passage to the surface, with Darius and Kasandra closely following him. Sweetbriar, curious as to why they had all just left so abruptly followed a short distance behind.

Emerging from the tunnel she saw they had stopped and seated themselves outside the entrance to Elderberry's museum. As she approached, they remained seated and gave her no greeting for they were all deep in thought.

"What troubles you good captain?" She asked.

"For over a hundred years this company has existed for one purpose, to find that which was feared lost, the humans' last hope. This was the mission set for us by Seamus himself all those long and many years ago. Well now that we have found it, we are faced with a far larger challenge ahead of us, what do we do next, where do we go from here, what is now our purpose."

"You don't have to go anywhere. You and your company can settle here and make this your home. And as for your purpose, help us to keep it safe. You said you were sworn to protect the late kings' lands and its people, so do exactly that".

"A generous offer, a place to call home. If your Lord Hawthorn agrees to it, then I shall gladly accept."

"He does" Came the voice of Lord Hawthorn who just walked up behind them along with Delphine, having left Elderberry examining the vault.

"Hurrah!" Sweetbriar exclaimed with joy "Welcome to

Greenvale".

As they chatted together excitedly Brasidas sent Kasandra back to the company to inform them they would all be back shortly. Then looking about at the building they were in front of he stepped inside for a look.

"This is where Elderberry keeps his artefacts, he calls it his museum" Sweetbriar explained as she accompanied him. Brasidas scanned the room. It appeared to him much like all the countless other ruined buildings he had entered, dusty chairs and desks were dotted about, old cabinets stood against one wall and there was litter everywhere.

"Doesn't look like much to me" Brasidas said at the sight of this jumble of junk.

"No not this, these things were already her, his collection is over there in the corner, see for yourself."

Approaching the items as directed, Brasidas saw the odd assortment of knick-knacks that Elderberry had unearthed. While clearly, they had been something of importance to somebody long ago, they seemed so trivial now compared to what they had witnessed in the vault. But then, just as Brasidas was about to leave, a ray of sunlight passed through the glassless window and reflected off the surface of a small item amongst the many. Stepping closer his eyes became transfixed on its tiny star shape and the symbol at its centre".

"It's a clover leaf" Sweetbriar explained.

"No, not clover, it's a shamrock, while I have never seen this before, its description is ingrained in the minds of all that serve the company, for this is the regimental badge of the Irish Guards" Brasidas responded, but as he did so, a sudden realization dawned on him, and he spun round to look again at the room he was in.

Before his eyes the room brightened and became as it once was. The desks were neatly arranged and the chairs clean, and his imagination conjured the ghosts that had haunted him all his life, but these were no longer shapeless faceless forms drifting like mist. There in the corner he saw Freya seated on her cushion, her paw placed gently yet protectively upon her precious toy. On the floor next to her was a shiny bowl from which she had earlier tucked into a hearty breakfast of biscuits and sausages. There also was Seamas and his friends, Sasha, Saxon, Butch, Sundance, Dutchess and Janey. In front of Seamus, Brasidas now saw her, the science lady, but now she had a face, and a name, Doctor Helen Fisher, and Brasidas heard her voice for now he knew the sound of it.

"Go with grace gallant captain, and do not let your love for us stay you from your course, for should you return, you shall find nothing here but death".

Brasidas dashed outside, and stopping at the entrance to the building he glanced first one way then the other. The trees and weeds that surrounded him faded from view and the ruins they'd concealed seemed to rebuild themselves. Twisted shards of rusty metal unfolded into the military vehicles they once were. Beyond them the lawn with many graves, and beyond that a stretcher party emerged from the door of the medical centre. Then, looking down towards the broken gate through which they had first come on their way up from Frosthome, he now saw it upright again and before it a single sentry stood dutifully awaiting any that should wish to pass. On the side of that little lane were a row of guardsmen ready to give Seamus and his team a farewell salute. Then the image faded from his mind, and the world of weeds and ruin returned to his eyes. He then found himself drawn to the remains of those old vehicles as if an unheard voice was calling him. As he approached, he looked closely at something that lay half hidden in the sprawling mass of undergrowth. There, lay the bones of a long dead human, and next to them were two red cans of the type humans would've used to carry fuel.

"Freya was right about corporal Smith, to his last dying breath, he never gave up."

Then, as Brasidas pondered the tragic fate of this poor fallen soldier, to his mind came a slow steady ticking sound. His mind raced back to his dream and there before him the clock upon the mantel piece. What did it mean? Had his dreams been trying to tell him something all these long years? Was there something hidden within the steady rhythm of this relentless tick tick tick. And suddenly, armed with new-found knowledge, the veil finally lifted and Brasidas began to laugh.

The others couldn't understand this sudden outburst of laughter for it seemed to be prompted by nothing at all. Darius had to ask.

"What is it sir, what's so funny?"

"I see it now; all these decades we've been blind to what was so openly staring us in the face".

"But what?" Darius continued, more confused than before.

"All through the years the company has tried to complete the mission Seamus gave us, but all the while we should've focused our attention on hers. Remember the science lady that told Seamus not to return. That was who we just saw on the screen in the vault. Seamus took her at her word and never came back here. All those years of searching yet he never thought to look in the very place he had left behind."

"But in that case, why did the humans have him take the key if the vault it opened was right here?"

"Because the mission wasn't to open the vault, but to ensure it stayed closed, at least until the time was right, for time heals all. If the vault had been opened too early its contents would've perished for the world was too sick to sustain such delicate growth. It wasn't hope for the humans she was referring to, for she knew they were already dead, but hope for the world itself. That's what she meant when Freya heard her say, time without us. It was human activity that had wounded the world, and only time without them could heal it. That's also why on the screen in the vault she addressed us as whoever or, more importantly, whatever we are. And as for our long hunt for this location, we could've come here anytime had we understood, for the answer was in the story all along. All the company ever had to do was return to the ruins of Wellington Barracks within the flooded city and retrace Seamus' steps back here.

"That means we have been wasting time on a long search that was never needed".

"No, not a waste, time was needed for the world to heal and that's precisely what happened. Time was never an item waiting to be found, it was marching along beside us every step of the way. Besides, had Seamus returned straight away he and his companions may never have formed the company, and it was their mission that kept us together long after they'd passed over to Wolfhaven. Imagine how the world would be without us, how many Cleon's would've ruled with impunity without the company to stand against them. How many innocent creatures would've perished needlessly without our protection. No, it hasn't been a waste of time, be proud of all we have achieved. But now, speaking of time, I believe it's time we returned to the company, I'll need to address them. Lord Hawthorn has a vault clearance to organize, and he will no doubt require whatever assistance we can provide. But you Darius won't be turning your paw to farming just yet my friend, I'm afraid you'll be too busy for that. When I address the company, I shall be announcing my retirement for my role is fulfilled. I was the last commander of the great hunt, and with that hunt now over, going forward the company shall be one of defence, and that task I pass to you. I was fated to be at the heart of the final chapter in a story Seamus began so long ago. I inherited the mission he set for us, but that is now complete, and a new future awaits. The company will need to adapt to a world without the hunt. For that, fresh command is required, and you Darius shall be the one to provide it. I hereby promote you to the rank of captain, effective immediately. With my resignation the company will be yours, good luck my dear friend".

"Thank you sir, it has been an honour and a privilege to serve under your command, it shall be a hard act to follow but I swear to you, I won't let you down."

"Of that I have no doubt." Brasidas replied, and glancing up toward the sky he caught sight of a large black bird flying way off into the distance, and remembered the chance encounter with the raven that led them to this place.

"If there flies the prying eyes of a raven, just think of the tale it has now to tell."

Then walking alongside one another, Brasidas and the newly promoted captain Darius, accompanied by Lord

Hawthorn, Sweetbriar and Delphine, they all headed down the slope towards Frosthome, but when they reached the old gateway, Brasidas halted them for he realised the importance of this moment.

"Time is like the ticking of a clock; the hands move ever so slowly forward, but eventually they come full circle and find themselves at the very point they first began. When Seamus and his team marched through these gates, the age of man was ending, and the age of the hunt began. That story has now come full circle, and its final chapter has concluded, precisely where it began. But the hands of the clock don't stop, they tick ever onward as a new age begins. That age shall now be your story my friends, and let it be a grand one, for here begins the age of hope".

And as they then proceeded through those weed covered posts where once a guard had held open the gate for Seamus and his seven companions, the ghost of that same guard now closed the gate of that final chapter behind them.

THE END

33: THE APPENDICES OF SWEETBRIAR

Carefully placing the last stick down beside the others, Juniper looked up at Rose and smiled.

"Well, those were the written words of Sweetbriar herself, what did you think of it? I hope I got the chapters in the correct order."

Rose chose her words with care so as not to offend.

"Well, I must admit I found it a bit confusing to start with, but it all seemed to make sense at the end, but speaking of the end are you sure about that?"

"Of course I'm sure, it has the tree symbol, see for yourself".

"No, I don't mean that, what I mean is, there's so much left untold. What happened next.,what about the seeds, what did the company do, and what about Brasidas after he retired? The story tells of great characters and events and then just snatches them away from us once we are hooked. I need to know more".

"I know exactly what you mean Rose. I too was eager to learn more beyond the chapters, and as luck would have it, Sweetbriar left copious amounts of notes. I have made a start deciphering them and these few here do answer some of our questions."

Reaching for the first of a few lose sticks, Juniper continued.

"This one speaks mostly of the seeds. It says that it was the field mice that were of most help for they instinctively knew what each one was and when best to sow them. Many lost fruits and vegetables returned to the world, so too did an abundance flowers. A land of plenty and beauty flourished over the course of just a few years. Strangely, to this land of colour even the bees and butterflies returned, though none knew from where, for the language of insects is lost on us. The birds also helped greatly, for they ate their fill of fruits and berries, and their droppings spread new growth far and wide. The world in which we live today is full of the life those dying humans left for us to enjoy."

"And what of the company?" Rose asked.

"Well from what little I've found combined with what I already knew, they adapted well to their new role as guardians of Greenvale, and in the years that followed their numbers grew. So much so that the scout team grew into a full-blown pack in its own right. Fenrir had initially been promoted to sergeant but eventually made lieutenant and became the first pack leader of this newly created reconnaissance pack.

Darius, as company commander, proved a dependable asset to this fledgling world, and would be only too willing to lend support to all that needed it. The wolf camp you know today at the lower end of the valley, is actually just a small detachment of a much larger contingent that owes its origins from the days of Darius and the company. This great army, with its headquarters based in the valley of the Faithful is now composed of several companies and has garrisons all over the land, still guarding our world and keeping us safe, even today.

As for Darius, he found a mate with Delphine and the two were wed. For this they travelled back to George's churchyard and were betrothed in the light of the golden man. In time they had two sons, the eldest of these, Darius named Phineus after his fallen brother. But in name only was the similarity between the two, for although this Phineus certainly possessed his own good measure of strength and agility, it was his kindness of heart and devotion to his friends and family for which he gained most renown. Darius' second son he named Spartan in honour of his friend, the first wolf to fall in the great battle. An irony not lost on Darius that he should name his sons after those two that had battled one another so many years before. This Spartan became fascinated by tales of his namesake and would spend much of his puphood in the company of either Fenrir and the other scouts that had served with him, or Sweetbriar, for she was the last to fight by his side. As he grew, his character developed so like that of the original Spartan that many said he had been somehow reborn in Darius' son."

"You mentioned George and the golden man, are they still there?"

"George, sadly not but the golden man still shines. It became a site of pilgrimage for many, though those that went were, and still are, always mindful to keep off the grass. A party of squirrels went to reposition the slipped tiles on the roof, and this became a regular visit by them every spring for any church maintenance required. There is even mention that on one such pilgrimage Chindit accompanied them, so we do at least know he recovered from his injuries. George's family still tend the grounds outside the church, and the oldest of them today is apparently the youngest of George's grandchildren. It's said he still remembers the time wolves came to visit, though being so young at the time he is scant on detail, so whether he is referring to Brasidas, Spartan and the other scouts, none can tell."

"And what did happen to Brasidas after he retired, what did he do next?" Rose was anxious to learn as much as she could.

"Well, on that score I have found very little so far. Only this short passage here, and sadly this refers only to his passing. It does not contain any mention of when this took place, so we have no idea how long after the events of her main story it happened. Nor does it mention the circumstances that led to his passing. It states that Darius was by his side as his strength left him, and it goes on to say that as Brasidas lay dying, he said to Darius "I have seen her; I have seen the face of my mistress. She shall be home soon, and I must be there for her when she arrives. Farewell my dearest friend". And to this Darius replied tearfully, "Go to her my brother, and may your dreams never end." and as Brasidas fell into the long deep sleep of death his tail wagged slightly as he went. And so ends the only mention I have so far found of Brasidas after the great events that led to the opening of the vault".

"And Sweetbriar, surely she mentions herself somewhere?"

"Ah yes, Sweetbriar, that brings us to the very reason you are here. I'm sure you have already guessed by now that this museum is the same one where Elderberry stored his artifacts, the very same building that was the headquarters from Seamus' time. Uphill behind this building you will even find the vault, long emptied now, and used only as a workshop for the guild of squirrel engineers that try to figure out the workings of old human machines under the dim light of candles crafted from beeswax. Why they would wish to work in such dark conditions is beyond me, but those engineers are an odd bunch at best. Many of the artifacts you'll find here have been gathered from all over the known world, but some were here from the start. By deciphering the story of Sweetbriar I have finally learnt some of their meaning. Over there you will find the ragged remains of Freya's toy that once contained the key to the vault, next to it sits her bowl from which she had her final breakfast before the great journey. Also, you will see the blue ball that Bramble threw to Trixie, the very same ball that once belonged to the human dog handler that threw it to the companions as they played. And there also you will find a great number of the regimental badges that were unearthed here. But if you wish to learn more regarding Sweetbriar herself then you must come with me."

Rose followed as Juniper led her towards the doorway at the back of the museum, but as he reached it, he paused.

"That large piece of wood upon which Sweetbriar carved her key was once the top of one of the old desks that stood in this building, there were several such desks if you remember."

And passing through the doorway, they entered a large room filled with many sticks and branches all carved with a multitude of pictographs, and against the back wall leant more of the remaining desktops each engraved with differing keys.

"The refurbishment of Frosthome revealed far more than just a single panel. I have deciphered only the first of these, and if we wish to learn more, we must read the rest, and now that you understand what the job I offer you entails, that brings us to the most important question of all, when can you start?"

34: EPILOGUE

The puppy lay comfortably at the end of the sofa. His blanket had been draped there and it was warm and snuggly. There was no sound to disturb him. He glanced up at the mantle and the candlesticks upon it. How long had it been, had the shadows moved across them at all. How long had his beloved mistress been gone, it didn't matter, if she walked through the door one minute after leaving, he would get as excited as if she'd been gone a week.

Suddenly his ears pricked up, someone was approaching the house. He leapt from the sofa and hurtled across the room to the open doorway. Mummy is home, he excitedly thought to himself, his tail wagging with glee. Through the doorway he bounded and along the hall. He could see the silhouette of her at the frosted glass window set into the front door. Then the sound of the key being inserted in the lock. It turned and slowly the door opened. Oh how exciting, his tail wagged even harder. There in the doorway she stood before him, and as he looked up at her adoring face, he saw his beloved mistress. Her eyes glinted, not with sorrow, but joy for seeing him.

"Hello, my darling Brasidas, sorry I've been gone so long, it seems like I've been stuck at the lab forever, but I'm home now and we can be together at last." She said sweeping him up in her arms and hugging him as his tail wagged furiously and he tried to lick her face. Then, with the devoted puppy in her arms, she walked through into the cosy living room.

"It's strange," she said "I have no memory of this place, nor how I came to be here, yet I know it to be home, and even though I think we have never met, I am certain my place is here with you, for we have a bond far stronger than the moon to the earth, and I know in my heart of hearts that I love you. Now, I suspect you've been a busy little boy yourself in my absence. So come my brave little captain, you can tell me all about your adventures, but there's no rush, we have all the time in the world."

35: ABOUT THE AUTHOR

Norfolk born and bred; I left school at 16 (that was normal back in the 80s) and went off to join the army, enlisting in the 1st battalion Royal Anglian Regiment in which I served for a few years before returning to take up a civilian career, although maintaining my military service with the territorial army. But now, with army life a distant memory and my civilian career drawing to a close, the time has come to focus my attention on more fulfilling pursuits. Living in a small riverside village in the heart of the idyllic Norfolk Broads, my wife and I both prefer the peaceful tranquillity of rural life over the hustle and bustle of the busy world outside our Broadland sanctuary, and it is here in the company of cheeky squirrels, boisterous otters and skittish kingfishers, I can turn my hand to painting, military history and growing vegetables in the kitchen garden. But my latest interest is writing. I may be an amateur, and this, my first attempt, may not be an epic read, but hopefully you've enjoyed it enough not to set the dogs on me. Nor a company of wolves for that matter.

Printed in Great Britain
by Amazon